CONSERVATIVE FREAK

Conservative Freak

Toni Rain

Toni Rain
Grand Rapids, MI

Conservative Freak by Toni Rain

ISBN (print): 978-1-7329310-2-2
ISBN (ebook): 978-1-7329310-3-9

Library of Congress Control Number: 2020911331

Toni Rain LLC Publisher
PO Box 7442
Grand Rapids, MI 49510

www.tonirain.com

Front cover illustration by Albert Pierre.
Back cover photos by Ashley Triêu.
Lace on cover designed by Freepik.
Book and cover design by Julie Taylor.

Table of Contents

What Is a Conservative Freak?

It is someone (whether a woman or a man) who goes about their business but has a strong sexual desire. They usually work hard, but "play" just as hard. Intimacy seems to be one of their favorite hobbies. Most tend to be in professional fields and are usually viewed as having to have a "polished" persona. Their "drive" is a part of their lifestyle and will be embraced like any other aspect of their lives. Conservative Freaks enjoy intimate adventures in places outside of the bedroom just as much as inside of the bedroom. They know that their lifestyle can be seen as "taboo," but live in their truths regardless of what others may think about it.

*Orgasms are cosmic euphoric masterpieces of songs
playing through the veins of your body.*

The Dugout

We pulled up to the park. It was a summer night and it seemed like every star was glistening in the sky that night. We both got out of our vehicles simultaneously. He smiled and reflected a smile back. His smile was just a tad bit wider than mine. We walked across the field, meeting at the metal fence that surrounded the baseball field. I talked about my love for softball. During my younger years, I was pretty good at being a batter. I guess you could say hitting balls was my thing...no pun intended. He went on to say that I probably couldn't swing to save my life. He had a way of being a smartass at times. He was loving, but he liked to joke around quite often.

I leaned against the fence and gripped it with both hands. He asked me to repeat my motions. I asked him, "Why do you want me to grip the fence again?" He told me that he liked the position that I was in. I told him to turn and look the other way. I wasn't intending to turn him on.

He asked me to sit and talk with him. The only place to sit in the area we were in was the dugout. We walked around the fence and sat on the bench inside of the dugout. We talked and reminisced about the fun that we'd had over the years. The topic of places we had been intimate in came up. We brought up the risky places we'd had sex in. He then came right out and said that he wanted to make love to me right where we were...in the dugout. I instantly got turned on. There was no hesitation on my end. I wanted it just as much as he did.

The first thing that I said after the invitation was "Do you have protection?" I wasn't even going to budge if he wasn't prepared to have me. Indeed he was prepared, like every other time we'd been intimate. It took no time before we began to kiss. His hand slipped up the back of my shirt. One by one, he unfastened the clips of my bra. My breasts slowly shifted downward and he grabbed them both. Again…he was prepared for me. His hands then caressed my sides. I leaned closer to him. I let him adjust himself before we proceed. Once he was settled, I straddled him. I left no time for games or hesitation. He was stiff as a bat. I mean…we were at the dugout. Shouldn't he have been? My rain was prepared to fall. Even though the sky above us was clear, there was a heavy rainstorm inside of that dugout. The precipitation was covering both of us.

Jerk

Pull me. Twist me. Tie me. Tempt me. Turn me into a Temptress. Let me ride you.

Let's play hide-and-seek. Touch me. Suck me. Spank me. Have my soul find you.

Cuff me. Bite me.

Just make sure that you jerk me…

Lunch Break

It was a typical day at work. Staff were smiling and greeting per usual. I gave the "Oh hey!" with the fake smile to make it look like I absolutely loved my job. I noticed that I hadn't checked my phone since before I'd stepped through the doors to clock in. When I went to see if I had any missed calls or text messages, I saw that I had a few notifications. Indeed, I had a few text messages. One was the common *Wyd* text; typically that made my mind immediately halt and think, "Next…"

There was one in particular that did catch my attention. It read, Hey Royalty. I hope that you're still wearing your beautiful smile that I put on your face. The sun needs to stay smiling on you all day. Now, for some reason, this message caused me to melt to my knees internally. In order to even be persuaded to pay attention to someone, I need to be treated as the Queen that I am…at all times. He had picked up on this immediately.

I had warmed up lunch, but I pretty much picked over it. I was swooning in my thoughts, deciding whether I was going to reply or not. I didn't want to fall off track. I wasn't going to let it be known that he "had me." Playing hard to get is best at times. I wanted to be a tease. I wanted to play in his thoughts. I wanted to be dangling on his mind.

As I was taking a forkful of my salad, another message came through from him. It read, I'd like to have you for dinner today. Wait a minute…that didn't come out right. I'd like to have you over for dinner. Get with me. At that very moment, I knew that later on he'd be tongue-tied.

Drinking Bowl

Make sure that you cuff the bowl with both hands.

While you drink it be sure to let all the fluids run down the corners of your mouth and down your cheeks.

If it hits the floor, just wait to clean it up later.

She Tried to Come for Me

So I went to an event to hang out with some friends. Once I got there, I was asked to set up some items and mix and mingle. I looked around the room and scoped out who was on the scene. I introduced myself to everyone present. I'm friendly like that. There was one person who gave me a different kind of look. It was one that I had experienced a few times in my life…and only a few. I gave the classic head nod and kept it moving.

I could literally feel their presence and them continuing to stare me up and down throughout the night. There was one particular time when I was talking to someone and they looked across the room at me and we made eye contact. Once again…I gave them the head nod.

Fast-forward to the end of the event. All the guests exchanged business cards. The one that kept staring at me throughout the night came up to me and told me how they liked my energy and couldn't get enough of it. They mentioned how they weren't from the city and how they'd want to connect with other people. They also brought up how they wanted to support my business and that they would be in touch. I didn't give it much thought.

A few days later, I got a text message notification. I was greeted with the *Good morning Queen* message. Another text came through telling me who they were and how they had met me at the event we'd attended a few days prior. It was the same person who had been staring me up and down and side to side.

I sent them a text message that said, *Good morning my fellow Queen.*

She began to text me saying how she wanted to get to know others around the city and to attend some events that were coming up soon. I went to my Facebook calendar and sent her information about what was going on in the city. She thanked me and stated how cool of a person I was for looking out for her.

I told her it was not a problem. She went on to tell me how she thought I was one of the most beautiful women she had seen. I thanked her and didn't think much of it. I receive and give compliments to other women on a regular basis. It's never in a sexual context, but just out of love and the desire to build up others. She asked me about an upcoming event. I told her that I'd be attending and she asked if she could join me. I didn't have a problem with it, so we arranged for a time to meet each other there.

I arrived and noticed that she wasn't there. I texted her, asking about her whereabouts, and she said that she was on her way. About an hour went by and I was restless, so I decided that I wanted to go back home. I texted her that I was about to head out. She told me that she was lost and asked if I could meet her at a nearby gas station before I headed home…just to talk to me for a moment. I felt bad for her being "lost," as she said.

Once I got there, I noticed a vehicle that was playing loud music. Come to find out it was her. It appeared that she was trying to set a "vibe." She had her trunk open so that her music could be even louder. I was a bit embarrassed because I didn't want the attention to be on us from the customers that were going into the gas station. I asked her if she was still going to attend the event and told her that I could give her directions from where we were. She was not interested in attending that event…like…not at all!

I noticed that she kept looking at me seductively and biting her bottom lip. I had been looked at like that several times…but from men. In my mind, at that moment, I knew that she was trying to set me up. She'd had no intention of attending that event. Her intention was strictly to attend me. She said, "I'm gone be honest. I think that you are gorgeous." She kept complimenting me over and over. I told her that I was tired and that I had to go home to get ready for the next day. She responded, "Damn, I feel like you're trying to dodge me right now."

I said, "Excuse me, but I made an attempt to meet you at the venue and you were late and couldn't find it."

She apologized and said that she hoped that we could hang out another time. In that moment, I felt a bit taken aback. I told her to have a peaceful night and that I hoped she would make it home safely. She wanted a hug and asked if it was okay for her to give me one. I said sure and gave her a hug. She tried to caress my back; then I said, "Okay, well, I'm about to head home now. Be safe."

The following day, I received more text messages from her. She complimented me on how nice I looked the night before. After the complimentary text messages, more and more started to come through from her. Now, mind you, she had mentioned at the party how she wanted to support my business, right? Well, nothing of the sort about her wanting to support my business came up during any of those text messages. Instead, what did come up was a total shock to me. These were text messages that I had never received before...well...from a woman.

She explained how she couldn't get me off her mind. It was brought up that she was bisexual. I told her that I didn't have a problem being with friends who were lesbian or bisexual. I also told her that I was only sexually interested in men. I received the *Well don't knock it till you try it* text. She asked me if it was okay if she proved me wrong. I told her that I wasn't interested and that we could just be cool.

I then was asked if she could send me some of her work to take a look at. I asked her what kind of work it was that she was referring to. I then received some poems via text message. I realized that some of the words were what she was saying to me and how she'd met me. I realized that she had written poems for me. My mouth opened and dropped. I couldn't believe what I was reading. She mentioned how she wanted to make love to me and how she wanted me to pull her hair while she had her face in between my legs.

I thought to myself, "What am I going to do about this woman? I don't want to hurt her feelings after she just poured her heart out to me and was open and honest with me."

I thanked her for sharing her work with me, but said that again, I was not interested in being with a woman. Her text messages went from her being friendly to irate. She felt that I'd led on her and that she had no interest in being friends with me. I was given an ultimatum to either be her lover or be nothing at all to her. I told her that I wasn't interested…once again. I never heard back from her.

Goldilocks

I arrive to you with my golden-brown skin and
golden twisted locks

You see me and grab me by the nape of my neck

My hair lies across your hands

I'm asked if I'm here to see Papa Bear to get some of
his porridge

I smile with delight

I'm told that it's nice and hot

I ask if I can stick and lick my tongue into the bowl
as if a cat were licking it

I want to taste the porridge right on the tip of my
tongue, to see if it's as good as it was the last time…

Fishnets

Walk into the room that I booked for us. I ask you to shower and clean yourself up for me. I lie down across the bed patiently waiting for you to come to the bedside, while you're slightly wet with water drizzling down your back. Your natural soft hair still feeling damp. You come over to me. You lay your head on my stomach. I slowly move each finger through your hair. I move both of my thumbs across your temples. I hear your silent sighs of relaxation. You are at peace. You lift your head, trying not to fall asleep. You look down at my love pillow as if you want to eat. You lift my thighs one by one. I'm wearing red fishnet stockings with the midsection open and available, waiting for you to satisfy me. You grab one of my feet and put my toes in your mouth. Your tongue is felt through the peeks of the net. Eventually you remove it with your teeth, then put my foot back in your mouth. You are staring at me as if you are a lion looking at a gazelle. By this time, my pussy is wet as hell. I feel "her" throbbing and beginning to swell. I want you to taste me while inhaling my natural smell. Take me. Kiss me. Caress me. I'm pulling on your hair as you take me all in. I'm hoping that no one hears me through these walls. I let out my outbursts, not caring about my yells.

The End Before the Finish Line

You can get all the intimacy and the emotional connections
before you actually get to that climax.

You do know that, right?

You can keep me full by your touch, your massage, the licking,
the sucking, and the biting of my nipples.

Me having my ass lifted to the sky while you watch the promise
of my clit; staring you in your face is enough for me.

My eyes closed while you have one hand moving and caressing
my body, the other wrapped around my neck.

My ankle rested comfortably over your shoulder.

You spank the sides of my hips, watching my thickness jiggle.

You bite your bottom lip while you watch me watch you.

I see your slight side smile when you catch me glance up at you.

Your shadow over me like a warm summer day.

I try to keep myself cool too,

So I suck on your stiff popsicle, letting my tongue quiver,
anticipating if you will melt down my chin.

I stop before I get to the taste of your center.

This is all good enough for me.

Zaddy Daycare

So I pull up to the coffee shop. I park my car, check my phone, then look in the rearview mirror. I don't see any vehicles that I recognize. I send him a message saying that I just made it to the location. He tells me, *I already see you. I'm right behind you to the side.* I look in my rearview mirror once more, then shift my head over my left shoulder. He is parked in my blind spot. I notice that he's looking in my direction. We both get out of our vehicles almost simultaneously.

I'm greeted with one of the happiest smiles that I have ever seen on a man. He says, "It's so nice to see you! Let me get a good tight hug." I hug him and the grip is so naturally inviting. It is pure. I don't think that it could get any better than a gentle but tight grip around my waist. But it does…in fact, it gets even better.

We sorta chuckle the sensation off and head toward the door of the coffee shop. We're greeted and asked what we wanted to order. At the moment we place our orders, he's immediately irritated and says, "Um…excuse me, but there is a fly hovering over the food in here." In my mind, I'm thinking that maybe it wasn't a good idea to meet up at this particular location.

We proceed to order tea, hoping to get a nice conversation in and catch up. There's an open table in the far back corner against a large picture window. He asks if it's okay to sit in this area. He knows how much I love the outdoors, which is why he chose this particular area of the shop. We talk, have some laughs, and then the irritation from him sparks up again. There are more flies…at least ten throughout the shop. I think to myself, "This is not going well."

But again…it gets even better. He says, "Come on. We're about to get out of here." I ask him if he wants to try another coffee shop and then go for a walk. He's like, "Nah, I have another idea for us. Let's go to my place and have tea time." If looks could talk, I'm quite sure that he growls at me in his head…but in a good way.

We end up leaving the coffee shop and I follow his vehicle to his place. Once we pull up, he quickly opens his house door. At first, I am a bit in my feelings because I feel that he should've walked to my car door first before opening his house door. I walk up to the house and he's standing there smiling at me. He says, "You may enter. A Queen should always come through the front door and never through the side or the back." I immediately get out of my feelings and then I am smiling from ear to ear.

I walk through the door. The first thing I notice is how comfortable and clean his place is. He shows me around and then I sit on the sofa. He asks if I want to have anything to drink other than the tea that we brought back. He mentions that he has spring water and wine. I asked for a glass of both. It's all good for the skin, so I insist on having it all. We both notice that it is starting to rain outside. I get up and look through the blinds at the rainfall. He stands right next to me and admires it with me. It is so peaceful for the both of us.

After a few moments, he starts to play some old-school music. He hits me with the ol' "I bet you don't know about this song!" I tell him that I'm literally a walking jukebox. He laughs it off and asks if there are any particular artists that I want to listen to. I give a few for him to play to vibe out to.

He asks for my hugs. This time the hugs are tighter and more caressing than they were at the coffee shop. In my mind, I'm like, "Oh shit…he better stop 'fore the rain really starts to pour around this house." The hugs then turn to him kissing me on the forehead, then on my cheeks. I slowly walk away, but I'm smiling as I walk away and start to look out the window again.

I then walk over to the couch. He goes into the kitchen to get something to drink. As he walks back into the living room area, he stops behind me while I'm sitting on the couch, still holding his drink in one hand. He has big, gripping hands, by the way. He's holding the drink in one hand and then he takes his other hand and tilts my head back to lie against the couch. After he tilts my head back, he takes my hair and slings it over to hang over the couch. He then moves my head toward the left, leans over, and softly pecks my cheek, then heads down to the side of my neck. He does this same routine to the other side of my face and neck. I close my eyes, laugh, and tell him that he is getting a little too comfortable. He tells me that it is his mission to make me as peaceful as I possibly could be and that he is willing to do whatever it takes for me to be in that space. In my mind I'm like, "Damn…anything?" I play it off as if I am not as into it as he is. I don't want him to think that I am a weak woman. But it does feel hella good to be in the space that I am in.

So I go to the restroom. As I'm sitting there, I'm contemplating what my next move is going to be. I don't know if I should leave or stay at this moment. While I'm washing my hands, I hear clinking noises and smell the aroma of seasoning. I think to myself, "Now, I know that this man isn't in there about to cook me something to eat?!" Sure enough, he is preparing lunch for us. He has even cut up beautiful and colorful veggies to make a salad.

He says, "So do you want ranch, french, or vinaigrette dressing on your salad?"

I reply, "Vinaigrette, please, and thank you."

16

Power

How can you hold that much power? Power in your dick. Power in your tongue. Power in your lick. Keep me tongue-tied. Keep my mind mesmerized. Make me your secret. Have me tucked and nestled in your thoughts. I want my soul to feel warm inside of yours. Make me your voodoo. Control me. I will control you. We make our seesaw. I pounce up while you pounce down. Sit me over your knees and spank me. Make me listen. I tell you to shut up. I grab your neck. You grab mine. You pull on my hair. I grip the top of yours. I put scratches on your back. You go deeper. We get lost in the power of each other.

When you see yourself as royalty, then so will others.

AssStroNaut

Him: Somebody has been keeping the mints away from me.

Me: You didn't want to be heated up and cooled down at the same time.

Him: I think that you're worried about me rearranging that backroom.

Me: It's not that I'm afraid of "him." I just want "her" to stay pretty and youthful as can be.

Him: Let me give her a little stretch tonight. I want you face down...ass up. You were ready the last time.

Me: She is always ready for some reason...it only takes a few seconds. (Even a thought will flicker her flame). But yeah...maybe I'll let you have your way one day.

Him: If those back shots hit right?

Me: I'm not a back shot kinda woman. You know what I like.

Him: You're about to be one that likes it. You will like what I make you like.

Me: Interesting. In all my years, I've never grown to like it.

Him: What time are you going to be ready? Well, mark the calendar, my love.

Me: I have preplanned arrangements for today and tonight. I'll be tired afterward.

Him: You'll find the energy.

Me: You'd like me restless and weak in my legs I'm sure.

Him: I want that backroom action. I'll record you putting in work tonight if you'd like me to.

Me: That's if I can stay up that late. There's always tomorrow, the next day, or the day after that.

Him: Leave early from where you are and cum see me.

Me: You are so controlling, you know that? It's cute though. I just might.

Him: Okay cool.

Me: If I'm too tired to make it back out tonight, will you still make some time for me either this weekend or next week?

Him: Yes, I sure will.

Me: Thank you, sweetie. Do you like spicy food? We could also go for a walk.

Him: I'm down for that. It'll also depend on the weather.

Me: We'll figure something out.

Him: We could also spend quiet time in one of our rooms.

Me: I'll consider it.

* * *

I end up hitting him back up a few days later.

Me: Good morning. So what time were you thinking for us to connect later this evening?

Him: Good morning. I want to respect your bedtime. How late do you want to be out until?

Me: I'm an early riser, so I don't like to be out too late. I'd say eight o'clock is reasonable for a lady like me. I have some studying and work to do tomorrow morning.

19

Him: Somebody might be a lil late coming in today. I have a few things to work on today. Afterward, we can get together, eat, and do some studying of each other for the rest of the day.

Me: No, I'm not going to be late getting in…you already told me that you were going to respect my time. Let's be reasonable with our time. But we'll catch up later.

Me: I was actually thinking about making today all about you. We can leave me out for today. If things take a turn, just know that a raincoat will suit fine…it's raining outside.

Him: Rain on the outside will make me wanna cum inside.

Me: You always have to have a rebuttal, don't you? Just bring raincoats, please and thanks.

Him: I know that you don't mind if I cum inside.

Me: We have to play it smart. Be nice to me.

Him: I'll try, but once the key is in the ignition, we seem to travel wherever we want to go. I'll be careful. But…I might let you drive and see if you can handle the steering wheel.

Me: "Pon da replay" huh? You want me to try my hand at driving? We shall see. But I'm still open to making it all about you. We'll see where the journey awakens us.

Him: Yeah, it's going to be an amazing session. We're going to take our time and enjoy each page of reading each other. We might have to read a couple pages twice to make sure that we don't miss any details. I'm not sure if you can handle steering from the passenger seat, though. We shall see. There may be a lot of turbulence during this rainy season. We have to be careful…might cause an early downpour.

Me: You want the small ocean wave to turn into a tsunami, right? We'll see if I'm going to stay in the passenger seat. I'm a driver, remember? Roles can be reversed and irreversible. Let's see who'll be the writer and who'll be read.

Him: My surfboard ready to catch that wave. Just because I put your hands on the steering wheel doesn't mean that you're in the driver's seat. You'll find out later exactly what I mean. You can be the writer…just don't forget it's my pen writing the words.

Me: I hear you loud and clear…she can hear you also. If I decide to let you use your pen, make sure that you only write in cursive. I want your manuscript sequential. Get yourself prepared for your tasks before we meet. I want you for most of the remainder of the day.

Him: My penmanship is great, but it's my hieroglyphs that'll have you speaking in tongue. I'll be eating fruits for breakfast, so you'll enjoy every drop of ink from my pen.

Me: You want to put your hieroglyphics in my pyramid…plaster my walls with your images. Being in a dark space, I will bring you light.

Him: What's written in stone will last forever. Place my name deep in your backroom so big that every time you squeeze your thighs my name will utter from your lips. An asstronaut traveling thru your yoniverse…call me Deep Space Nine.

Me: I like the fact that you can keep up with me with your wordplay. Let's see if it'll be like that in other areas. I'll be ready for you soon.

Head Strokes

He fucked me without fucking me. He rubbed his head temple against my head temple. He asked me, "Can you feel that? Yeah? Yeah. You feel it." He then moved his head away from me at a short distance. He slowly brought his temple back to mine and began to rub them together again. He did this action three times simultaneously. I felt every vibration that went from the top of my head to the bottom of my pelvis. From my pelvis, those vibrations moved down to each tip of my toes.

The Tub

After a long day of work and having an emotional breakdown, he calls. He hears the pain in my voice. Instantly he drops everything that he's doing and says, "I'm coming over." I hear the door open about ten minutes later. At this time, I'm sitting in the tub with dried tears on my face. I don't want to talk because if I do, I will probably start to cry again.

I hear the entry door close and shortly afterward, I hear the bathroom door crack. I can tell by the slowness of the door opening that he's taking his time with his approach. We eventually lock eyes. No words are spoken…just a few seconds of staring. He takes off his coat, his clothes, and his shoes right there on the bathroom floor. He strips down naked. It is a tight fit, but he sits behind me in the tub and caresses my arms (soft strokes). He kisses the nape of my neck. He puts his arms around me and puts his head against my shoulders.

We are now talking and an hour goes by. The water temperature changes from hot to lukewarm. I lift myself from the water. My ass is now in front of his face. He starts to place soft kisses onto me. All the while, I can feel his hands gripping my hips. The hands go from the hips to the thighs. Outer thigh to inner thigh…inner thigh to the pussy lips. All of a sudden he pulls me back to him. One foot overlaps one leg that's in the water. The other foot overlaps the other leg. My body is facing forward while he remains seated below me. I make a slight head turn to the right. My peripheral vision sees him staring at me. I turn my head again to now face forward. I look down and see his "Happy Partner" standing at attention. I make a slight smile, then squat on top of him. Small thumps are all I feel against my vaginal walls. I sit stagnant so that I can feel his fullness. I let a few seconds go by.

He asks, "So what are you going to do with him?" I say nothing. My knees begin to move forward. I wiggle on him. I make the muscles of my "Inner Core" grip his "Happy Partner" as much as I can. I release myself. Grip again. Release myself. And I repeat a few times more. I lift myself, letting the ripples and the splash of the water hit the inner sides of the tub. I hear him moan. He grabs my hips again as if he doesn't want me to move anymore. I lunge my hands toward the front of the tub while they lie under the water. I move my hips up and down, left to right. Up and down. Left to right. I repeat these actions. I stop. I stand. I turn my body around and put my feet on the opposite sides while I stand over and face him. Our eyes lock. No words are exchanged. I can smell the scent of nag champa incense burning in the air. My eyes are focused on his. I bend my knees, slowly bringing my body to connect to his. I make the connection to his. I make the connection from my "Love Lady" to his "Happy Partner." I place one of my hands against his shoulder. The other hand then moves to grab the back of his neck. My eyes are still interlocked with his. I lean in to kiss his lips. While we're still kissing, my lower body is still slowly grinding against his. In my mind, I imagine the water crashing against the tub walls as if all the oceans and seas are surrounding the two of us.

They say that you attract who you are. I am music. I am a song. I am a tempo. I am a rhythm. I am an orchestra. I am a hummingbird. I am a poem. I am art. I am love.

Colors

Wondering what colors I'm going to see tonight

I heard that I was one of a few that can actually see
the colors that I do

Every moment of ecstasy brings out different hues

Sometimes it's a burst of yellows, other times it's
blues

Each time it's a psychedelic experience

It's almost as if looking into the sky on a cosmic high

Another galaxy is where I end up landing

Never standing on my feet

This floating experience is different every single time

One after another the explosions intensifies

I'm one of the lucky ones who is granted this sort of
satisfaction every single time

This pleasure is all mine

In His Mother's Driveway

We arrive at the location almost simultaneously. I get out of my vehicle. He gets out of his. I walk up to him and ask, "So are we going inside the house or are we staying outside?"

He says, "Nah, we can get in my whip."

I'm like, oh…okay cool. I ask him what he needed to talk to me about. He proceeds to reach in his car, take some items from the front seat and back seat, and move them to the trunk. All while he's shifting things from one area to the next, I notice the music playing. I compliment his musical taste. I tell him that I'm used to us typically hanging out with some type of sports program being on the television. We almost never listen to music when we hang out. Tonight is definitely a much different space than I am used to. I like it. In fact, I love the whole vibe of everything. The night is crisp and cool, but not too cold. I'm seeing the moonlight.

It is a weekend, but the streets have very little movement. There is very little movement on his mother's street also. I ask where everyone is. He says that some are in the house, some are away, and some he hasn't heard from. We proceed to talk about work and friends that we were recently socializing with. A few laughs slip in. It seems like forever since the last time we were able to link up with one another.

I came over to the house dressed sexy, but not too revealing, as I typically am when I see him. While sitting, my legs begin to cramp up. I cross my legs and alternate the location of my posture. He asks if I am nervous. I tell him how my legs are cramping and falling asleep from sitting so long. He asks if I want to sit closer to him.

I say, "Of course I would be delighted to be closer to your person." He gives a slight grin. I tell him how it is surreal that we are sitting so close to one another again. Remember…it has been a while since the last time we were able to be side by side. In fact, it has been years since we were able to be in a space with just the two of us.

He slowly swipes his fingers across my right ear. I'm looking directly into his eyes as he's stroking my ear against his hand. Per usual, I give him a little smirk and look to the left. At this point, I'm looking outside the window, trying to throw off his focus. I lean in closer to him and proceed to move my body over the top of his. I'm not fully on top of him. I'm more leaned over his body, with my shoulders leaning against the window while continuing to stare out the window, adoring the night's sky. I see a few cars parked on the street, but not really paying any mind.

He then grabs me by my hips and says, "C'mere."

I say, "Come where?" (while smiling at him). He tells me to stop playing. I sit on his lap and kiss both sides of his cheeks. I talk about how I can't believe we have the night to ourselves. The entire time I'm sitting there…on top…of him. He then goes to reach to touch my ass. He moves his hands up and down, then says, "Where are your panties? So you just gone come over here with no draws on and sit on top of me like it's nothing, huh?"

I laugh and tell him, "Well, I wanted to be comfortable. That's how you want me to be, right? Comfortable??"

He gently kisses me and moves slightly snug under me, so that my back is lying down against the back passenger seat. Next thing that I know, my feet are now touching the ceiling of his vehicle. I can hear him pushing the button to let the window down. At this point, it's hot in the back seat. I have my eyes closed most of the time.

Then I hear, "Oh shit! My brother just pulled up."

I panic for a moment; then he put his hand on my stomach to lay me back down. He wants to finish, so I let him…even while others are inside the house and some even parked on the street.

Channels

Turning the knobs.

Turning the stations.

Anticipating which channel I'm going to watch next.

Who my connector leads me to awaits behind the
lines.

Me going in the direction my energy leads me.

I have no control.

It's already pre-programmed.

They wait their turns to be turned on.

The vast emotion that is to be.

No one has control.

No one has consciousness.

We are all one.

We are all connected.

The program is programmed into different channels.

Your Highness

Him: Royalty is exactly what you are, my beautiful Queen. Is there a desire present for me inside of you? I'm trying to put some paint where it ain't, sweetheart…you feel me? You winked at me earlier…I thought that the door was cracked. Give me the rules as if I don't know. I'll tell you some things about me that I like and enjoy. I love smothered potatoes and onions cooked in olive oil with pink Himalayan salt and pepper. In case you'd like to know, I also love pineapples. I like tea tree oil and clove oil…I put it in my diffuser. Yes it's a battle…for the simple fact that we're learning ourselves daily, which makes it much more of a challenge to learn someone else daily. It's bittersweet being single. It has its ups and downs…lonely periods. Women can lack consistency and can be borderline shallow. I keep to myself a lot. You begin to learn more about people and their intention. I don't like energy-suckers. As long as you're good to me, I will treat you well.

Me: I love to love more than anything. I just love to love on people in general. I feel that there's not enough of it going on. I like journeys and adventures. I love being outdoors and nature walks. But when it comes time for cuddling and eating good food with my man, I make sure that I find time for that…always. Home always comes first.

Him: Teamwork is to be inspired as well as inspire. Creativeness and confidence…I'm sure I went out of the box…but I was just naming some things. Are you making me a dating profile or are you just trying to get to know me?

Me: No, I'm not making you a profile, silly. I'm trying to learn you.

Him: See none...hear none...speak none. I want you to know that what we discuss is what we discuss. Nothing goes outside of this conversation box. I'm very observant. I think that you're starting to know who I am. Do you feel my energy all the time? If you do, then rain on my parade.

Me: See...you're trying to wake me up it looks like lol. I'm going to keep ducking and dodging the subliminal messages.

Him: I don't mean no harm...I just like to have fun.

Me: You got teeth, right?? So basically you will still bite.

Him: What's on your mind?

Me: You're on my mind. You just so happen to be there, sitting comfortably on my mind.

Him: I'm adventurous along with being spontaneous. Don't be hesitant about me...I'm a gentleman...and I don't bite or hiss. I mean no harm...your aggressive gesture made me smile...I was feeling that.

Me: I see that you picked up on my aggression. I'm very aggressive and controlling, but most times there's still passion and spontaneity behind it. I'd actually say that I'm a professional when it comes to my aggression. I'll keep it at that.

Him: I'll read in between the rest. I want to learn you in every way. I will find all the spaces of you. I will read the book of YOU.

Me: Don't skip any pages and read each sentence until you reach the periods.

Him: Most definitely...I always do. That's the only way you'll get an understanding and a good reading. I don't like skimming. I want to read everything. You'll see.

Me: You can keep up I see. I have to shower and attend a dinner meeting. You're throwing my focus off. I'll get back to you soon.

Him: That was refreshing…thank you. I needed that crispness and breeziness from you.

Me: You're welcome, sweetie. My energy felt that you needed my attention.

Him: Tell me something good. So share with me this interest/appetite that you have for me.

Me: God be with me right now. I don't want to answer that.

Him: I'm all ears lol. Answer it as someone else then.

Me: I'm not "Crazy Carrie" with multiple personalities. What do you want with me?

Him: A cracked door to slip in. I want whatever your energy can handle.

Me: You're smart. I have to be careful with you.

Him: What do you want with me? Why?

Me: Interest. I want interest with you. I want a growing friendship with you.

Him: Great answer…I'd like the same. Why do you have to be careful with a friend?

Me: I felt your energy last night. I felt a lot of it. I mean…it really came out of nowhere.

Him: I felt the same. But why do you have to be careful with a friend??

Me: How much? What was in your thoughts?

Him: Quit dodging…lol.

Me: What did I do? lol

Him: You're dodging. Why do you have to be careful with a friend? You got me over here cracking up.

Me: I just told you, silly. I feel your energy too much. But at the same time, I am supposed to make you happy and smile.

Him: Oh, okay, but back to what you were saying about being careful. For that reason you have to be careful??…Careful of what?

Me: Your energy is more sexual than from a friendship standpoint, which is why I have to be careful with you.

Him: Oh, okay I get it now. My apologies for the lack of misunderstanding on my part.

Me: Am I right?

Him: You may have a point but it's yet to be determined. Only you know the true answer to that.

Me: I'm still learning you. It's quite fun actually.

Him: You haven't been around me, so how can you say that it's sexual?

Me: I'm an empath.

Him: I'm sure. You must find me attractive.

Me: I'm attracted to you as a friend…friend.

Him: I understand…you don't have to keep saying that "friend" word, unless you're trying to make yourself believe it.

Me: I think it's the second part.

Him: You know what it is. You can't run from emotions. You're an intelligent woman.

Me: It's hard for me to lie.

Him: Me too. I'm one authentic brother.

Me: I can feel it.

Him: Can you really?

Me: Seriously I can.

Him: I believe you. Something had to turn you on in regards me. Random question...do you burn sage?

Me: Absolutely and absolutely. I love incense vs burning candles.

Him: I like to burn sage. I do it primarily on the weekends to help me relax.

Me: This is crazy, but in a good way.

Him: What's crazy??? How much you're feelin' me?

Me: Haha! Be quiet.

Him: If you keep hitting brick walls, then you're only going to damage your hands. Don't fight the feeling...just walk into it. Let it flow naturally, sweetheart. Do you listen to music often?

Me: Why are you doing this to me? Yeah, I'm kinda spoiled in a sense when it comes to music. I couldn't breathe without it. Music flows all through my soul. It's part of my being.

Him: Good...it matches your deep passion. You are music to me.

Me: Thank you. You are always so polite to me.

Him: I've been a music fanatic since I was in grade school. I have jam sessions every blue moon. I like all genres of music. By the way, I made a bomb Sunday dinner...I love to cook. You'll have to try some of my meals. I guarantee that you'll come back for a second plate.

Me: Nice, sir. I love to see a man maneuver his way around a kitchen. There's something special about hearing those pots and pans click that does something to my heartstrings. I personally think that men cook better than women. You're more patient and take your time with things.

Him: I'm very patient and take my time with things...nice and slow. Do you feel me? I mean do you really feel me?

Me: Umm, I'm about to walk off.

Him: Walk where? Where do you plan to walk off to?

Me: I'm going to bypass that last part. Ahem, so what time do you intend on having tea time this weekend?

Him: I'm available all day...I'll let you decide. You are in control.

Me: You like me spicy and to be controlling over you? Don't you?

Him: Lol...no...just confident.

Me: Okay, I can be confident...and posh.

Him: How long can I have you?

Me: You mean how long can you have my time, right?

Him: Yes.

Me: I'll play things by ear, but more than likely most of my day will belong to you.

Him: You have me over here "cheesing" so hard. My smile is stretched from ear to ear.

Me: ...but that's if the planets are all in alignment. I'm glad to put a nice smile on your face.

Him: Of course. Things will play out how they're supposed to.

Me: I'll behave on the first hangout. Promise.

Him: I'm sure they will be aligned. You don't have to, but okay.

Me: I'm very blunt. How many women are you currently sleeping with?

Him: 1 every blue moon. That's it.

Me: Okay, thanks for letting me know.

Him: Where did that come from? What about you?

Me: I just want to be in a safety zone.

Him: Mos def.

Me: I currently have 2. One I haven't been physical with in months and the other we're trying to work on building with each other.

Him: Oh okay. Transparency is the best.

Me: Yes, I'm very honest.

Him: Me too. What else would you like to know?

Me: So what's the story behind your situation? Why is it that you only see each other every blue moon?

Him: We're doing the long-distance thing.

Me: That's sad. The ones that you have the strongest connections with aren't in arm's reach.

Him: I guess…if that's how you wanna put it.

Me: Would you rather them be closer or are you comfortable with the distance?

Him: I like the distance.

Me: Oh…well, just put myself back in my place then lol.

Him: Why do you say that? You're in a place of your own…like no other.

Me: No no no. I meant like, "staying out the Kool-Aid and not knowing what the flavor is" lol.

Him: Oh okay lol. Do I put a tingle in your wingle?

Me: What do you think? A straight-up mess is what you are.

Him: You turn me on also.

Me: I do??

Him: Your energy…sex appeal.

Me: It's 90% mental and only 10% physical touch.

Him: Very true. I certainly agree with you on that.

Me: I mean when you think about it, most of our communication is mental. I already know that you've made love to me in your mind. I felt it already.

Him: Wow…you're amazing. It's probably because you have done the same thing with me too mentally.

Me: I feel EVERYTHING.

Him: Did you feel me missing you over the weekend?

Me: Yes I did. You were working on "space and distance" and not wanting to overstep boundaries. You wanted me to miss you. It worked. Are you ready to throw your phone yet?

Him: No, I'm not throwing it yet. You throwing it?

Me: So you still gone hang in there right by me?

Him: Yep. Riders ride out.

Me: I'm controlling, so driving can be good for me.

Him: I'm sure. You imagined kissing me.

Me: How did you know?

Him: You might have more to talk about than you think. Like the moisture I create beneath the waist.

Me: It'll be more so based on the connection that we have. I've seen most of what I need to see in my thoughts and from what I've felt below. See…I read you again.

Him: Indeed. I guess you really can feel my energy.

Me: All the time. So did you get to see your long-distance friend this weekend?

Him: No I haven't. It's really sparingly.

Me: Awww that sucks. So what do you do for your personal release?

Him: I rub one out.

Me: I got you. Meaning that I understand.

Him: I know…you don't gotta always clear things up.

Me: I just had to clarify myself. I didn't want you to think that I was trying to be her substitute.

Him: You are funny. Tell me something good.

Me: I'm sweet like a…never mind.

Him: Peach or pineapple?

Me: Mango.

Him: Papaya is sweeter.

Me: Someone told me that I tasted like an "Airhead" piece of candy once.

Him: Wow!! Full of flavors!

Me: I guess so. Never had him inside of me. He only wanted to dine…for years. I actually prefer it that way.

Him: Who does that??!

Me: You'd be surprised.

Him: I see. Are you a pleaser? I am…I like to please and be pleased.

Me: It's more the other way around. I attract those that want to do most of the work. I'm like a jungle gym to them.

Him: Do you like to dine?

Me: It depends on the person. I never really had to. If I'm feeling it, then I will.

Me: Every man that I've ever encountered fell in love with me. I'm just putting up a warning sign for you.

Him: The long-distance thing can just become exhausting.

Me: I'm sure that it can become very exhausting.

Him: You come off as a very solid woman.

Me: Thank you. I can't live in a lie.

Him: What do you want to do to me?

Me: I already did what I wanted to do to you…in my mind. I already told you that.

Him: Ditto.

Me: So you already did what you wanted to?

Him: Yes Miss Lady.

Me: Was it good? Was it mentally satisfying your thirst? Did I make you cum like a Starburst?

Him: Yes your attention.

Me: Good.

Him: How was your day?

Me: It's been breezy thanks to a newfound friend. Do you know him?

Him: You better believe it.

Me: I want to stay connected to him. He's a powerful man.

Him: I feel the same, Queen.

Me: He was able to tap into my spiritual realm, which is hard for most to do.

Him: I have a certain aura and vibe that's priceless.

Me: I see and feel no lies.

Him: So maybe we'll be butterflies (lines from an Erykah Badu song).

Me: Quit making me smile so hard.

Him: Your energy feels so damn good to me.

Me: Thank you, sugar.

Him: I like sugar.

Me: I'll use it more often.

Him: It tastes good also.

Me: Yes, just like brown sugar mixed with cinnamon.

Him: …and mangos.

Me: It just might.

Him: So what would you like to do if I were to invite you over to my spot?

Me: I'm pretty simple when it comes to an invite. As long as there is music, a captivating conversation, incense, good eats, and maybe a glass of wine, I'll be good.

Him: Okay, mental note. Music, scents, food, and wine is right up my alley. That's the normal at my place.

Me: Yes…be sure to have the good conversation ready. Good good conversation. Sounds relaxing.

Him: I wouldn't have it any other way.

Me: Yes. Don't deny your cravings.

Him: I feel like you're breathing more life into me.

Me: That's what compatible energy produces.

Him: I'm realizing that more now. Thanks for the confirmation.

Me: Glad that I awakened that third eye on the subject.

Me: You better make sure that it stays open, too.

Him: No doubt. If I didn't feed your mind then what good would I be?

Me: Lol so now you gone use one of my lines on me, huh?

Him: Lol I knew that you would catch it. That was a classic line you laid out there.

He sends me pics.

Me: If you could see my face right now. You look so damn delicious, man.

Him: Thank you.

Me: You're trying to have me give you my "two scoops."

Him: Lol! …and then some.

Me: I'm gonna run from you.

Him: Just make sure you're wearing skates, so you can roll back.

Me: I seriously had water in my mouth.

Me: I feel like a female last dragon. I definitely feel the glow right now. It's heat coming from underneath me too.

Him: Fire…panty-liner ruined, huh?

Me: A bonfire.

Him: All I ask is that you don't bite or growl at me. I'll keep my paws to myself too.

Me: If I were to cut you off completely, it'll be an overwhelming feeling that'll come over you. That's what feelings are.

Him: I keep those in check, sweetheart…I'm not new to this. I'm true to it.

Me: Yeah, that's what I hear you saying. We'll see. Scientists are still trying to figure out what breed I am.

Him: They're trying to figure out the same about me.

Me: I already have you figured out. Tell 'em to come see me.

Him: Ha! So you say…

Me: I tried to warn you.

Him: Surface…not core.

Me: I feel that you know it in your core. There is a plethora of women that you can choose from, but you want me.

Him: You're on point, Queen. All of those women don't come close to your being.

Me: I think that you want me to sting you a little.

Him: I wear OFF

Me: Try using Citronella burners around me…OFF won't work for you. I have a test for you.

Him: Okay. Let's hear it.

Me: Can you go the rest of the week without any communication with me? Until Saturday?

Him: Yes…but I would still speak because we're friends. But if I have to I will…dry until Saturday. Watch me prove my point.

Me: Okay. Talk to you next week.

He hits me up.

Me: I knew that you couldn't do it.

Him: What did you want to prove by that test?

Me: You miss me, don't you?

Him: Lol I'm just asking.

Me: The point that I wanted to make was that it'll be hard for you to get me out of your system. I haven't even touched you and I'm walking around in your mind all day and night. I just want you to be careful with me.

Him: I'm always careful and I could still go until Saturday, but I was curious as to the reason for the test.

Me: Yeah, yeah, yeah. Okay. It's too late. You should've asked that yesterday lol.

Him: Yeah, I know…but I forgot and the reason was on the brain on and off.

Me: Keep playing and I'm going to be hula-hooping in your mind soon.

Him: Lol you're funny. I have mind control, sweetheart.

Me: I don't believe you, but okay.

Him: How did you sleep?

Me: I didn't get much rest. Hopefully tonight I'll get some sleep. I'm free tomorrow, so maybe I'll rest then.

Him: Save some energy for me.

Me: If you insist.

Him: Then after that, you're "man down"? I'll let you shower and rest.

Me: I'm unsure. I'll go in the direction that my energy leads me. I know where it's leading me in my thoughts. I hope that it stays that way. I think that you know too.

Him: Nice plan.

Him: Hey, honey.

Me: Hey, sweetie.

Him: How are you feeling?

Me: Working, peaceful, and listening to music. How are you?

Him: I'm watching the rain.

Me: You're working?

Him: Yes I am.

Me: I'll be watching the rain shortly…on break. Lucky you.

Him: I'm ready to go today. It's the kind of day that makes you want to just lie down and watch TV. Was the vibe what you were expecting when we hung out?

Me: Yep absolutely.

Him: My T-shirt smells just like you. I'm glad that I was able to make you comfortable.

Me: I'm sure that it was the best aroma that Michigan ever made. I appreciate you more than you know. Why do you do that? You're trying to make it hard for me, huh? You always look delicious.

Him: I could've done a better job stroking that pussy.

Me: You can't talk like that lol…so naughty. The jam session we had was something else. You didn't know hardly any of the songs. I won.

Him: If you didn't have to get up early, I could've done a jam session all night long.

Me: Me too. I literally jammed myself to sleep.

Him: Rocked you right to bed.

Me: I felt that we didn't have enough time. We'll have to have another jam session soon.

Him: Same channel, same station??

Me: You know it.

We then start discussing investment options, stocks, and bonds. He tells me to check out some "buy ins."

Me: Thank you so much for sharing this with me. No one has EVER done that for me before. I've asked a few people to help and they never have.

Him: I feel like whatever we spend our money on is what we should be investing in.

Me: That's crazy how much we think alike. I invest almost all my money into the things that I'll need to be financial stable in...especially for my future.

Him: Good...all of which may not yield tangible dividends at the moment but the chances are greater with multiples.

Me: Yes sir. I'm listening. I just pulled my chair up to the table (metaphorically speaking).

Him: Unfortunately you were unable to see the many dimensions of me due to horniness.

I laugh.

Me: I noticed that too. You seemed like you needed some nice warm hugs.

Him: I sure did.

Me: I did too.

Him: How are you this morning?

Me: I'm great. The weather is perfect and things are going well. How are you feeling?

Him: I'm good…sunny day.

Me: That's always good.

Him: You good?

Me: Yes I'm good. But…I did decide to not overwhelm you.

Him: Why?

Me: Not trying to overstep boundaries.

Him: You're not…what would make you think you were?

Him: Didn't I bring out a side of you?

Me: Yeah, one that I tried to keep hidden. Adventures are the biggest highs.

Him: Me too.

Days later.

Him: Hey, honey.

Me: Hey, suga plum.

Him: I miss those kisses.

Me: What kisses?

Him: Oh okay…yeah…what kisses?

Me: You're a wild boy. You need an "around the way girl." I'm too far, sweetie.

Him: How are you this morning?

Me: I'm having a rough one, but I have business to handle.

Him: Awww, poor thang. I'm good…over here starving…can't wait to eat.

Me: Yes…I need a lollipop to help me feel better.

Him: Caramel one?

Me: Yes…or butterscotch.

Him: Was that a request? You want me to do you?

Me: You know telekinesis right?

Him: I wish.

Me: I'll let you figure out my response. I think that you're comfortable walking through fire. You must have feet of brass.

Him: Yes…absolutely I do.

Me: Stop it lol.

Him: I'm supposed to go fishing, but the weather ain't having it.

Me: Yeah it's raining over here too. It didn't rain until last night. It's due to global warming I think.

Him: It's due to something…'cause it hasn't stopped.

Me: Soon we will be like Washington State. It's always raining there. Also, it can cause more people to fall into depression…a topic that's taboo, but needs to be discussed.

Him: True baby. Very true. May I have some hot tea?

Me: You always know how to get to me. Why are you doing this to me? I'll be back. I have to go to the restroom.

Him: Make sure you hang them up and let them dry.

Me: I'm running from you, man.

Him: Now why would you do that?

Me: Am I not one of the first people that you think about upon your awakening? If I wanted to visit you every week would you let me?

Him: What you having for lunch today? Yes I would.

Me: If I wanted to come over just to rub on your head, would you tell me no?

Him: I like my head rubbed and you know this.

Me: If I wanted to give you a reflexology session would you push me away? Okay, I'll stop now.

Him: Yes…I loved that…that was the shit.

Me: That was just a snippet. I'll have you feeling as peaceful as a monk messing with me.

Him: Yes, I'd like that.

Him: The other day, I tasted your juices then hit my cousin's J. He tasted your lips too.

Me: You better stop playing. I keep thinking about how I'm going to handle your crazy behind.

Him: You were there…did you forget?

Me: I was in my own world.

Him: True…but you knew what I was doing to you before he got there…and I'm sure you smelled the reefer.

Me: No…meaning it didn't dawn on me that you didn't go to the washroom, silly.

Him: Oh okay. Gotcha. I had you all on my top lip.

Me: Oh my goodness, you are a mess. You're nasty and your cousin is nasty (even though he didn't know it) lol. I bet that you won't tell him what you did?

Him: Nope.

Me: Damn.

Him: Mangos.

Me: I'm whooping you.

Him: You liked how I was smacking that ass.

Me: Smacking what ass?

Him: Oh yeah…that wasn't you. That was someone else.

Me: Stop making me laugh.

Him: You laugh harder when you're trying not to. That's what makes it funnier.

Me: You're not right. You want me to make as much noise as I can.

Him: You're right, naughty girl. I wanna throw your legs behind your head again…on the ottoman. Did you cum??

Me: What are you talking about? Your imagination is on a whole other dimension. You must have a big dream-catcher hung up in your bedroom.

Him: I wanted to suck on that pussy right on the ottoman when you spread eagle.

Me: You got my hands shaking right now. You wanted to suck and lick on me the moment we met…off jump.

Him: No I didn't.

Me: Right. What made you want to originally?

Him: All a part of seduction pleaser.

Me: Sounds like you pleasing is your ultimate pleasure.

Him: It sounds like it can be yours as well.

Me: Perhaps.

Him: Good answer.

Me: Thank you.

Him: You miss me, don't you?

Me: I think that someone is trying to put their thoughts and feelings on to me.

Him: No…just asking.

Me: I have to use NDA tasks with you.

Him: What's that? Non-disclosure Agreement?

Me: Yes.

Him: That's all between me and you, baby.

Me: Trying to get me in a "Charlotte's Web."

Him: Never.

Me: I'm still going to have you sign one.

Him: I'm not messy, sweetheart…I just like to have fun. Just bonds and memories we share.

Me: I know. I like to have fun too, but I have to be careful.

Him: I got your back, baby.

Me: You better.

Him: I'm solid, boo…not flaky. I'm a fun guy, baby…not messy or no drama. When it's over, it's over. I'm a different breed.

Me: Guys have done some shady shit in the past. I'm just being careful.

Him: No bitch-ass-ness…real men don't play hoe games, baby. I got your back through the mud.

Me: I'm still rocking with you.

Him: Likewise.

Me: I will put you on a good punishment if you have small slip-ups, but not for major ones. The whip will be coming out. Did I make myself clear?

Him: Crystal.

Me: Good.

Him: Ready for the boat life later…wish you could join me.

Me: Woot woot! I would like to go for a ride today. A boat ride that is…

Him: Come on down.

Me: I'd like to, but I have plans for the day.

Him: I like to make you smile.

Me: You always do…even when we're not in communication.

Him: Oh really…I didn't know that.

Me: I'm glad that you know now.

Him: Hey, honey.

Me: Hey, sweetie.

Him: I wonder if you're yearning like I am?

Me: What do you think?

Him: What do you feel?

Me: You tell me what I feel.

Him: You said you feel me, so I wanna know what you feel?

Me: I'll tell you verbally one of these days.

Him: Why wait?

Me: I will say that those that were once attractive to you will now irritate you more because they're not me.

Him: How else will I know? Confident and cocky, I see.

Me: More than anything, I can feel your irritation for not being able to touch me.

Him: Not irritated…just yearning.

Me: Eh…a slight difference. I'm supposed to be fasting, remember? I'm trying to fast from being "fast." I'm also trying to avoid either one of us falling in love with each other.

Him: The distance does a great job of that already.

Me: No…not really.

Him: Yes it does. Or we would have seen each other by now again.

Me: It's still early.

Him: You're strong enough not to fall.

Me: I am. You aren't. I don't like to play with people's emotions anymore. I used to have fun doing that, but it's not morally right.

Him: I'm strong enough…trust me, it's not new to me. You're not playing with me for the simple fact that I already know the situation so therefore I react accordingly.

Me: I hear you too. It's not new to me either, but the ending is always something completely different.

Him: It's a dry suitable ending when everyone acts accordingly. Not to mention a great secretive bond that was formed.

Me: So when I'm in that area the next time and I don't see you, you'd be good with that right?

Him: Sure…will you?

Me: I'm on the fence.

Him: So…you're thinking of not coming to see me? I just want to make sure we're on the same page, sweetheart.

Me: I just don't like playing with people's emotions. That's all. I'm still going to be in your area. Maybe we can meet in a public location to keep things neutral.

Him: My emotions are intact and controlled. But okay. So you're pulling back already?

Me: Will meeting at a location work for you?

Him: Once again, I just wanna know so I can pull back also. I just wanna always be on the same page...an understanding is the greatest thing in the world.

Me: We both decided to pull back a few days ago, remember?

Him: Whatever floats your boat. If that's how you want it...I'll follow.

Me: I'm just trying to figure out the right move...for both of us.

Him: Positive aura. But like I said...I'll follow. I like that refreshing feeling. The fact that you're not always available keeps it fresh and new.

Me: I'm opposite, though. I have to have interpersonal contact to keep interest.

Him: In my case, I have to be happy with what I can get. I like interpersonal contact as well...but you're the leader in this situation.

Me: If I was the leader, you would visit me weekly, sir.

Him: Ohhh...now the truth comes out about if you were the leader or not lol.

Me: Sometimes...the master becomes the student.

Him: True.

Me: Just like in a book, character roles switch around in different scenes.

Him: I would have never imagined you'd say every week.

Me: Scenes change. I make time for what I want.

Him: What scene are we in?

Me: If you want to keep up with me, I'd advise that you set aside a "Travel Fund Account" (TFA), because one of my requirements is interpersonal communication.

Him: Travel Fund Account…lol…okay.

Him: It's funny you say that 'cause I have that same attention disorder as well.

Me: So what will it be?

Him: Ask yourself…I applied the first invite to another state to hang out. Trips and voyages are a must.

Me: I never declined.

Him: I know…I'm just putting it out there. The same way I put it out there when you were lying down in my bed. Sometimes you have to get fed to understand.

Me: Why do you insist on playing so much?! You and your daydreaming again. Anyway, I already had your trip on my "to do list."

Him: You're amazing by the way…just wanted to share that with you.

Me: Thank you my newfound lost friend.

Him: I wasn't lost…your eyes weren't open.

Me: You cut a slither in them and made a pathway with beautiful flowers. A beautiful disaster.

Him: …Flower Bomb.

Me: Yahtzee.

Him: Yes, baby. I think that you were missing me yesterday. For the record…I was missing you too.

Him: You ever have a yoni massage?

Me: No, not professionally.

Him: So you're quite familiar with it? Well…I possess that talent.

Me: It's nice to be thought about from a guy like you. I'll keep that in mind.

Him: Have you seen videos of it done professionally?

Me: I had a yoni massage from someone from another country. I thought they put a "root" on me. It felt amazing!!

Him: From the looks of it, mine will blow your mind.

Me: The one that I had did blow my mind. The best part is that I didn't have to have sex with them.

Him: I've done it twice before. They teach it in massage therapy, but it's not legal in the U.S.

Me: No, it sure isn't legal in the U.S. I just might have to schedule you in for an appointment.

Him: I've never seen a woman have back-to-back orgasms like that until I performed those yoni massages. But okay…pay more for happy ending lol.

Me: Yeah, that's cold work. I don't need intercourse to be fulfilled. I need very little of it.

Him: Especially after a yoni…you should be good for a while lol.

Me: For at least two weeks. About how many orgasms have you had in the last few weeks?

Him: I know your seductive ass gets it regularly.

Me: No. You'd be surprised.

Him: I hit a lick this morning.

Him: How many times did I make you cum on my couch? Or was I always making you stop too soon?

Me: God be with me right now.

Him: I'd like to know…that way it makes it better next time.

Me: Would you stop?

Him: Okay.

Me: Thank you.

Him: Lol…thank me later.

Me: Omg.

Him: "I grabbed her by the throat, but I didn't choke her. Just kissed her so deep she forgot whose air she was breathing." — Unknown

Me: That's very seductive. How did your dentist appointment go?

Him: It went well…no cavities. Just cleaned and polished.

Me: Yay to no cavities! Even with all the sugar that you've been eating…

Him: Are you referring to the brown sugar and honey that I've been intaking?

Me: That could be a possibility.

Him: How are your studies and working coming along?

Me: I've been busy, but I like being that way. If I'm not productive, then I feel that I'm not whole. So do you use a hi-lo for most of your work?

Him: Front-end loader is what I'm in all day…every day.

Me: Ohhh…so you ride a CAT all day (no punt intended).

Him: Yep…ride the hell out some cat.

Me: "They're Grrrrrreat!" as Tony the Tiger would say. Both of my parents created a masterpiece of artistry.

Him: Mine too. That's why I like you.

Me: Thank you. I guess we've got something in common.

Him: Quite a few things.

Me: I start singing "Something in Common" by Bobby Brown ft Whitney Houston.

Him: I miss them lips.

Me: What lips, sir?

Him: I miss both.

Me: You don't say?

Him: Are you doing a good job of keeping your mind off me over there?

Me: I was until one of my coworkers brought up how LL Cool J licks his lips a few mins ago. Then boom! You popped up in my head. Tell me 3 things that I don't know about you. They could be anything.

Him: I played basketball in school. I want to go on a cruise. I also love to be on the water. I know 3 things about you. You're warm-hearted, busy body, and you love the limelight.

Me: Eh…I like being in the background more than anything, but the other two are right.

Him: How are you feeling?

Me: I'm feeling really good. How about yourself?

Him: I'm good, just ready to see you.

Me: I'm ready to see you too. I'm not going to plan a time or a day for when I'm going to see you. I'm just going to pop up.

Him: Does that give you a sense of power?

Me: I always have the key. I'm a female sensei.

Him: Ma'am. Yes ma'am.

Me: Oooh I like that.

Him: What are your plans for Saturday?

Me: I have one event to attend. Are you going to the lake?

Him: No, I'm not going to the lake.

Me: What are you doing?

Him: Nothing planned.

Me: I'll have some down time coming up soon within the next month.

Him: Oh okay...I know that you're glad about that. A brother is missing you, that's all...nothing major.

Me: I might turn down a few streets and come swing your way. I miss you too.

Him: Why am I yearning for you?

Me: Why do you think it is? What did I do to you?

Him: It's the energy mainly. We clicked outside the sex.

Me: What sex? But yes...definitely amazing energy connection.

Him: I miss hearing your voice as well.

Me: I miss my friend and talking to him.

Him: Him right here.

Me: Lol you want to talk now?

Him: Him downstairs.

Me: Hush lol.

Him: Yes, if you can.

Him: You must be Southern California. It's plenty of rain in Southern Cali.

Me: I thought that it never rained in Southern California??

Him: Yes it does because that rain had my chin soaking wet.

Me: Cut it out Mr. Gingerbread Man.

Him: That's Mr. Peta Man.

Me: The cookie and cakes man.

Him: Pattie Cake, Pattie Cake.

Him: I see that you like to hang around the deep dark seductive ladies. I can tell by your personality and swagger.

Me: Yeah that's the "tribe" that I'm a part of.

Him: I've always dug that tribe.

Me: I'll just put the tip of my fang in to see just a lil blood…not too much.

Him: I bet. I have leather skin, so I'm not sure if you'd be able to make your way through to me.

Me: It'll hurt so mother fucking good though.

Him: You should've rode me on the couch…just a random thought.

Me: Pounce on the cushion, huh?

Him: Hmmmm yeah. Yeah…cushion all right.

Him: This attention is golden right here.

Me: Okay good. I'm sure that isn't easy for you to do, especially from someone as sweet as you.

Him: How are you today? Have you been out in the world looking sexy and succulent?

Me: I'm sitting in my dress with makeup and jewelry on with my belly full. I just ate some delicious food. It most certainly wasn't as fulfilling as you though.

Him: I miss your face.

Me: I want to go on an adventure.

Him: Sex in the woods by the creek or water?

Me: It sounds fun with "whoever" you decide to go with. I want you to surprise me.

Him: I need our peace. I was wondering if I could enjoy the different attractions of you.

Me: You just may get a centerpiece put on your table.

Him: On a table or on an ottoman…it's your choice. I hear it's good for stretching and posture.

Me: Nice. I practice those techniques almost daily, so it shouldn't be hard to do.

Him: I'm young but at the same time, I'm a seasoned vet.

Me: Practice makes perfect. I do it to keep my legs and joints tight and strong in the case I have to run into the "Cookie Monster" or run from them.

Him: Run right into his arms is more like it.

Me: No, no, no.

Him: Panties just disappear.

Me: They can get mistaken for licorice sometimes.

Him: True. Mango licorice. I miss you.

Me: I miss you, Emperor.

Him: That title holds lots of power.

Me: That's because you're a powerful man. You'll realize it soon. Goodnight, sweetie.

Him: I can dig it. Good night, queen.

Me: I've been balancing so much. I need a break from everything.

Him: You're going to need reflexology, 'bout time you get still, mama.

Me: You know what? You might be right. Relaxation needs to be put in my planner too.

Him: No doubt.

Me: I left my schedule open for the next weekend, so who knows.

Him: Me and you hopefully. Pencil me in.

Him: My sugar is low. I need some sweet mango.

Me: Do you need "Sweet and Low"? Cane Sugar? Or simply... mango?

Him: Mangos only...it's summer time.

I start to reconsider our situation. I'm not sure if we should continue our communication.

Me: I don't like complicated situations. I deal with a hectic work schedule and life. My outside world has to be as mellow as they come.

Him: I gotcha.

Me: A breakup...and we don't even go together lol.

Him: Why do you give up so quickly? With our energy, I believe that we can make anything work.

Me: I've exhausted myself with false hopes and heartbreak, so I run away from it. If things start to shift, then I tend to walk away from it.

Him: "We've only just begun…the romance is not over. There's so much more to give."

Me: That's Glenn Jones!!

Him: Aye…you know it?! I had no idea that you were on to his music.

Me: You can't hit me with the classics! You're not playing fair.

Him: Energy, baby…never forget that. It's all energy…you can't run from that even if you wanted to. You feel me?

Me: I will never forget yours. Promise.

Him: So you're serious? 'Cause I'm down to do whatever for us to see each other.

Me: I'm not looking for a summer fling. When I put energy toward someone, I give my soul. I don't give it to just anyone. I want a forever thing…nothing temporary.

Him: I'm the same way, baby. I'm a vibe and energy follower.

Me: On a scale of 1–10, where do you think we are as far as that? How much room do you feel that needs improvement?

Him: I think that our chemistry is an 8 only due to our availability for one another. As far as improvement, I can only take what I get given, that you'd like to move slow. I respect your pace. How about you? What do you think?

Me: I was seriously going to say an 8. It was all natural and organic. There's no forced energy at all…even from first sight.

Him: I know, right…you're something special.

Me: Even your hugs were impeccable. I miss those.

Him: The chemistry is one that should not be denied so soon.

Me: I'm fighting myself internally. I did try.

Him: You can't resist what feels good.

Me: I'm learning that. I can run all I want, but my spirit will bring me back to that connecting line.

Him: That was deep.

Me: Thank you, love. I speak and write how I think. I'm glad that you felt that.

Him: How was lunch?

Me: It wasn't anything fancy, but it's one of my favs...oatmeal with fruit and raisins. How about you?

Him: Side salad...Italian dressing. I love oatmeal...with green apple chunks and cinnamon.

Me: No way...get out of here. I don't know many people who like oatmeal. Oh yes, I love cinnamon in mine too. I've had salad the last 3 days.

Him: Do you eat dates?

Me: Why, yes I do, sir.

Him: I was about to say...'cause you sure ate your date a couple weeks ago. Haha! Will I hear your voice today?

Me: Haha! You are so not funny. Yes, I'll call you at "never o'clock." I had to get you back lol. I'll call you soon.

Him: Smile...someone is thinking about you.

Me: Thank you, sugar. I miss you.

Him: I miss you too, baby.

Him: Pack a bag.

Me: Quit trying to plan my weekends.

Him: Shit…I was trying to plan your today and forever.

Me: So in other words, you want to see me all the time?

Him: I was hoping today. I ain't seen you in weeks, so I'm basically
ready any day. I need my temples rubbed.

Me: Yeah I bet.

Him: For real. Plus I think that you're about ready to be seduced
again.

Me: You need some Zen in your life. I'm that fresh air and balance
that your body is craving.

Him: Do you always have the right words to say to me?

He contacts me the next day.

Him: How is my brown sugar doing today?

Me: I'm yours now? I'm impressed with how you're trying to mark
territory. I just finished making my dinner. After I eat, I'll rest,
then it will be bath time.

Him: Make sure that you get your relaxation time in, so that you'll
have energy for when you see me.

Me: I don't have an appetite anymore…for food.

Him: Oh okay…what do you have an appetite for?

Me: Well, maybe a little something sweet. Like…butterscotch. Just
one piece. Not too much.

Him: Oh okay. Sweet tooth, huh?

Me: Just a little.

Him: Why not a lot?

Me: Probably because I still have some thinking to do.

Him: I have a slight crook in my neck. I may need your help with getting this kink out.

Me: You know that I got you.

Him: Okay, see you soon.

Him: Good morning, honey bee

Me: I promise not to put my stinger on you. Good morning, Emperor.

Him: You already did.

Me: I did?

Him: Yep.

Me: My hands are tied.

Him: Did you lose your dominance?

Me: Never. You said that you wouldn't waste my time. I literally felt that.

Him: I took care of that.

Me: Yes, absolutely.

Him: I like the way we click.

Me: It's easy and natural (never forced).

Him: I really needed to hear that.

Me: Namaste.

Him: So did you get your fix until the next time that we link up?

Me: Like Smokey's momma said on Friday, "Make it enough." I have no choice. I feel like I've been found.

Him: When were you lost?

Me: I didn't know that I was in the lost and found until some months ago.

Him: I found you?

Me: Someone did.

Him: Here you go.

Me: I'm not sure. "We attract what we fear." I read that somewhere.

Him: You think so?? What do you fear?

Me: I think that my biggest fear is abandonment. I didn't realize it until I became an adult. What is yours?

Him: Mine too.

Me: Are you just saying that jokingly?

Him: No…I'm serious. I hate being ignored or brushed off.

Me: I apologize for yesterday. It's exactly how I felt was being done to me.

Him: I always feel people should speak their mind first before throwing shade. Especially when y'all have a regular vibe and energy.

Me: You're right. I've been working on myself. I used to shut down for weeks, months, and years. I'm learning to be more self-expressive.

Him: Transparency is the best way to be.

Me: I agree wholeheartedly.

Him: Reason being…none of us are mind-readers.

Me: I am. Reason being for me is that I can't let love in or give it out when I'm in shutdown mode.

Him: How does that make you feel when you do that?

Me: What? Me shutting down?

Him: Yes. Cold?

Me: It's a defense mechanism. I've had a lot of trauma, so I shut down when I think that someone will either physically or emotionally harm me. I know that not everyone means harm. I realize that everyone moves at different speeds. Some don't put value on others as much.

Him: I see. Play it accordingly. You want to be guarded, but at the same time, know that there is still love in people.

Me: I'll try. To be honest, we got comfortable quick. It threw me off a lil.

Him: Where did that come from?

Me: I didn't have enough time to run from you.

Him: Is that normal?

Me: Is what normal?

Him: Running.

Me: Yes. I can't live the lifestyle that I want to live.

Him: Understood. Will I have the chance to hear your voice this evening too? I can call you on my break if you're available. You always gotta keep a lil game involved..."'cause once love walk in the game walk out. She has your number and that's where you fuck up."

Me: I'm just letting these words ponder. It's something to think about. I've never heard that before. You always put me on to some kind of old-school game.

Me: "Love is a hell of a drug."

Him: Sho ya right. On that note, let me take a shower. I miss you.

Me: I miss you too, sweetie. I was listening to a song that said, "Come over to my place and put a smile on my face." I was hip-rolling in my chair while sipping on some juice.

Him: Rollin like Saturday…Rodeo style.

Me: One of my friends gave me some bomb-ass dragonfruit and strawberries.

Him: I need some dragonfruit.

Me: I love it.

Him: I was talking about you.

Me: Great minds. It's a soft fruit and light in taste.

Him: Sweeter than mango? Does sugar have a long way to catch it?

Me: Shut up lol. My friends have been spoiling me for some reason lately. They've been treating me to some of my favorite fruits.

Him: I just bet. I need me a massage.

Me: So does that mean that you need to go see a massage therapist?

Him: Nope, you handled that the last time. As a matter of fact, you handle it every time for me.

Me: How is your neck feeling?

Him: A lot better. That pain didn't stop my action though. I always handle business no matter what.

Me: Yeah. You kept pushing that train. Choo choo!! You are freaky in your own way. It's tucked inside of me and folk is trying to pull it out.

Him: Yes ma'am. Indeed you are right.

Me: I'm more seductive than freaky. I guess that you can say that I'm more so in the burlesque category (look but don't touch most times).

Him: Exactly…teasingly freaky.

Me: Yahtzee

Him: Lol.

Me: I'm like that toy that just came out, but it's not really meant to be played with. Just set me on the stand as an antique.

Him: Lol…until I take advantage and you submit.

Me: You help my day go by, honey.

Him: Likewise.

Me: I went to one of my favorite parks today with a few friends. I think that I belong in the wild. I believe in reincarnation.

Him: Fly free, butterfly.

Me: You are so sweet and romantic. Good morning, Emperor, with your handsome self.

Him: Why, thank you, sweets. How are you this morning?

Me: I was able to see the sunrise this morning. So far, it's been beautiful. How is my friend doing this morning?

Him: That's wonderful…I'm good on this midweek hump day.

I send him some old-school gangster rap.

Me: Sending good good old-school vibes your way. My vibe for today.

Him: Aye…old school gangsta joint…NWA and Too Short was some of my first gangsta rap listens. Honestly, Too Short wasn't a gangsta rapper, he kicked that pimping.

Me: Yep!! I like all of them. Too Short was always played at my mom's spot, so she put me on the pimp game lol.

Him: Lol…dig that.

Me: I'm still trying to figure out why you want me to be one of your select few.

Him: Same reason why you want me to be…energy, vibes, and connections.

Me: Touché actually.

Him: There you go.

Me: Do you want me to speak in a foreign language when I'm with you? Or will English be just fine?

Him: No…I wouldn't understand what you're saying.

Me: Right on, brother. Right on.

Him: …but the way that you're set up…you like that kinda shit. Stuff like that turns you on…to be able to mesmerize someone with foreign wordplay.

Me: I'll only use a few words here and there. My facial expressions will help you with the meanings.

Him: I'm sure. Fuck faces.

Me: Peek a boo.

Him: "I see you." (In my "Martin" voice on "A Thin Line Between Love and Hate")

Me: I love that line. I know exactly what you mean. You miss me like I miss you.

Him: You must feel it.

Me: All the time.

Him: Tell me about it. Winter time can take its time.

Me: I'm not thinking about Old Man Winter. He can stay gone for all I care.

Him: I'm in need of our overnight jam session.

Me: I want one of those too. I will make it happen. Aye dirty wind on dem.

Him: Dig dat. I can't wait to eat.

Me: What do you have for snacks?

Him: You. Nothing other than that.

Me: You better stop playing. You need 6 small meals per day.

Him: Yep.

Me: When you can't sleep, what do you usually do?

Him: Toss and turn or I hop on the damn phone. I need to find some other hobbies.

Me: Do you think it's because you want to be caressed at night? You should be journaling and meditating.

Him: You're right…I should be doing something other than getting on the damn phone. I need to finish reading my book that I recently purchased.

Me: Yeah, you need to detox from time to time. I mean…shut down the devices and turn off the TV.

Him: I'm going to take your advice and do that.

Me: Thank you, honey.

Him: But how on earth do I reach out to you if I do a detox?

Me: That's what detoxing is. It's hard, but necessary for mental cleansing. You will be just fine without me for a few days. Are you sad?

Him: No, baby…why would I be?

Me: Okay, just making sure.

Him: It's easy when you have a mate…but when you're single with nothing to do, it makes it harder.

Me: I understand. That's why I say that some situations need more than one person in the house. You'd never be bored if you were around a certain individual.

Him: True. Could that individual be you?

We both decide to get tested for STDs. We show each other our results.

Me: I need touch on a regular to stay intrigued. Not intercourse, but massages and hugs.

Him: I know how you feel. I'll take whatever I can get, baby...I'm learning patience also.

Me: Okay, I'll think about it. One of my friends told me that I had a different look. They said that I was glowing like somebody was making me happy.

Him: I told you that you were glowing...you be "cheesing" harder.

Me: Someone else mentioned it besides you, so I guess it's true. Did you know that the penis could reach certain chakras of the body?

Him: What are chakras?

Me: Chakras are spiritual centers of the body, there are 7 of them. "Chakras are the circular vortexes of energy that are placed in seven different points of the spinal column, and all the seven chakras are connected to the various organs and glands within the body. These chakras are responsible for disturbing the life energy, which is also known as Qi or Praana." — Google Search

Him: Now that's a lesson learned. I never knew that. You're always schooling me, baby...that's why I like you so much.

Me: Sex is natural medicine.

Him: Oh word? I never thought of myself as medicine.

Me: From my experience, not all men know how to hit certain chakras, so if you do know how to tap into them, then you deserve a round of applause and a standing ovation. You are so sexy to me. You don't have to try either.

Him: I sure don't look it today.

Me: Why do you say that?

Him: I look rough today.

Me: It's not just the outward that I see. I see all of you.

Him: Thank you, baby.

Me: Kiss kiss.

Him: Give me a heads up before you go on a hiatus from me.

Me: It'll be after I come down there on that Mon. For at least a week, sweetie.

Him: Cool beans.

Me: You will be fine.

Him: I'll just revert back to 2 months ago…before the connection.

Him: Yes, that's what I'm going to "try" to do…8 more days. (meaning until the next time he would see me again)

Me: On the 8th day…he rose again.

Him: Boy did he.

Me: Lol.

Him: He then sends me a quote that says, "The happier she is, the nastier she is."

Me: Ain't that the 11th commandment? Just kidding. What is your weight/size preference for women?

Him: I prefer my lady to be thick. The curves, the thick thighs, and the hips are what I like.

Me: Okay…good. I love your response.

Him: I've been missing my sugar.

Me: Oh stop. No you don't.

Him: I'm not a liar.

Me: I'm just teasing. Thank you, honey. I remember you saying that women aren't often consistent. What did you mean by that?

Him: It's because they like to be chased.

Me: Do you like chasing?

Him: Kinda…but not always. I'm thinking about a career shift. I know that was off topic, but I wanted to put that out there.

Me: I think that you get a lil thrill out of chasing.

Him: I do.

Me: If I was available, you probably wouldn't want me.

Him: Not true at all…it's your personality and spirit that I like. I'll never judge you off your personal situations or your financial status.

Me: Perfect. I like your response. I'm happy that I peeked around the door and saw you standing there waiting on me.

Him: Me too.

Him: I'm eating white cherries.

Me: Hey…I just brought cherries last night. Did you peek in my refrigerator?? I just caught up with some work, so now I'm feeling relaxed.

Him: I'm relaxing also.

Me: Okay, I'll let you chill. I miss you.

Him: I miss you too, baby.

Me: Hey, sweetie. Good morning. I'm about to shower and get ready for work.

Him: Good morning…okay.

Me: How is my friend doing on this lovely Friday morning?

Him: I'm great. I appreciate you asking.

Him: How are you?

Me: My funky behind is doing all right lol.

Him: Lol…why you say it like that?

Me: That's how the old folk used to say it lol.

Him: Yeah…you act old lol.

He sends me pics of himself.

Me: Sexy Papi. You're trying to make me miss you more. It's working. Delicious ass. You are wrong for doing me like that.

Him: Sorry to bother you, Queen.

Me: You are never a bother. I want all that energy.

Him: Take it then.

Me: I want to take more.

Him: How much?

Me: At least 50%. I'm spoiled.

Him: I'm quite sure you're getting that now.

Me: I know our situation won't allow it. It's something I'm mentally trying to prepare myself for.

Him: Oh really? Sure you are. You're getting 50% or better now.

Me: How? Not from you.

Him: Yes you are baby.

Me: I want your 50% remember? I'm talking about the physical included.

Him: Distance and time factors into that. It's something that is unavoidable at this moment.

Me: I want to smell and sniff you too.

Him: I know…I miss that.

Me: I want to have my nose right under your chin.

Him: You like that don't you?

Me: I love it.

Him: I thought that you did.

Me: I heard a line in a song that said, "You spend time with him, but I'm yo baby…."

Him: Dig dat.

Me: Truth hurts sometimes.

Him: Is it truth? I'm thinking about stepping out tonight. (he sends me info on an event)

Me: That sounds like a nice time to me. Send pics if you do go. I know that you will be looking cute.

Him: That's if I even go…I'm so stale.

Me: Stale as in how? Personality or style?

Him: I don't do much. I don't mind being a homebody.

Me: That's the best way. It don't take much.

Him: True.

Me: I want you to enjoy yourself. I'll be thinking about you in the meantime.

Him: Awww…how sweet of you. What time will you be coming to my place today?

Me: I will get there around 8 p.m. I'll stay until midnight. Or I can stay for a few hours since you have to get up early.

Him: I thought you were staying the night, baby?

Me: I can. I didn't know if you want me there while you were gone.

Him: I need you all night.

Me: Are you sure it's a need and not a want?

Him: It's both…and I get what I want, baby.

Me: Oh…so you're cocky now? Don't have me in the guest room acting like a stranger.

Him: I'd never treat you like that.

Him: So…you know that we're vibe and energy feelers right? Your vibe and energy is not mine today. I know my honey by now.

Me: You're right. I told you that I don't trust most often.

Him: My energy never changed, baby…I had a long week at work and once I got still, it was over. You have all my attention if you only knew.

Me: You're not on punishment just yet. I have a forgiving heart…too forgiving at times. Hold tight until next week. I give breaks, when I feel it's necessary. No kisses for you today though.

Him: Dig dat, but I'm sad about it.

Me: You'll be all right.

Him: What's up with you this morning?

Me: I'm currently doing my morning workout. Once I'm done, I'm going to shower, then head home. No plans for today, besides me having a massage scheduled. It's my rest day.

Him: Oh okay. Yeah, same here. I'm just relaxing.

Me: Did you party yourself out last night? Did you get on the floor and show them what you got?

Him: No, I came home by midnight. I was tired. I had been moving around all day. There was a party and I pretty much stayed in the house. I was buzzing and it was humid and mosquitos were vicious. I took my ass home.

Me: Okay, I gotcha. It's uncomfortable when it's like that. The spot that I was at was too hot as well.

Him: We're both going to need reflexology after that session that we both had.

Me: Sure ting, brethren. I got you if you got me.

Him: No doubt. I owe you.

Me: Thank you. Only 5 more days until we see each other again.

Him: Yes ma'am.

Me: Kiss kiss. I'm tired now. I'm about to shower and get ready for bed. Have a peaceful night.

Him: Yep…you too.

Me: Thank you.

Him: Guess what?

Me: What's that?

Him: I miss the hell out of you.

Me: I miss you more though. I'm trying not to catch feelings too hard. I don't want to mess up the situation.

Him: Doubt it.

Me: Old Man Winter keeps popping up in my mind, then reality settles in.

Him: Oh okay. Only 4 more days.

Me: It feels like I haven't seen you in months. Why do you think that is?

Him: …I feel the same way. This connection that we have is something else.

Me: It almost feels heavy not seeing you.

Him: True.

Me: I had a massage yesterday, but it's nothing like a yoni massage. I want a yoni massage soon.

Him: I got you.

Me: Friday or Saturday?

Him: Whichever day you want it…you want it pre-sex or post?

Me: Uh…pre-sex and I want it on Friday.

Him: Okay. You get what you want.

Him: It feels like I'm waiting on Christmas.

Me: I bet that it feels like you're about to open up the big box because you know that it's going to be the best gift ever.

Him: …and it ends up being a pair of socks in that big-ass box.

Me: It might only be some socks or it could be empty.

Him: Lol exactly.

Me: Either way, you will still have a box that you can reuse.

Him: Yeah…a juice box.

Me: Always that…Juicy Juice.

Him: …and I'm the baby. I want my Juicy Juice.

Him: Do you miss Daddy?

Me: I do. I most certainly do…more than I should.

Him: Really? Why do you say stuff like that?

Me: I'm just being honest.

Him: …and I felt every bit of it.

Me: It just took me by surprise. I didn't know that it would be so strong. I hate not being able to see you.

Him: I know…but like I said before, the distance will suppress the appetite. But…yet keep the yearning strong at the same time.

Me: It's my loving…AND I WANT IT NOW!

Him: My thoughts exactly. Don't run this time. Promise me that.

Me: I don't plan on it.

Him: Just making it clear…you've flopped on me before.

Me: When? I don't recall.

Him: Aww shit…I can't call it.

Me: You're about to lie?

Him: Nope. You fell forward from that thang, like you had enough.

Me: I'm so lost right now. I'm not catching on.

Him: Lol. I bet.

Him: What's on your mind?

Me: I'm prioritizing some things in my life. What's on your mind?

Him: Wow…my thoughts also.

Me: What are some areas that you need to work on?

Him: Playing catch-up in some areas. For example…credit cards. I'm also waiting on my transcripts to begin this apprenticeship.

Me: That's a major one. I had to the same thing a few years ago. I'm now on the right path. If you need advice, let me know.

Him: That's why I haven't been doing much. I stay focused much better that way.

Me: With credit cards, it's all about the utilization. As long as it's no more than 30% of your balance being used, it'll increase. You can also ask for a balance increase a few times out the year to help with the percentage. The next time that we have a sit-down, I can explain it more in detail.

Him: Oh yeah…I know about it oh too well. Creating more streams of income is the goal.

Me: Okay good. You're doing right by watching your spending and staying home. But there's always free events for you to attend (art exhibits, museums, etc), so keep that in mind too.

Him: Yeah, you're right. I gotta get all my time in with you before you go on your hiatus.

Me: It still won't be enough for you, though, sugar. You will forever have a sweet tooth for me…your whole life.

Him: Lol you are so silly. You think?

Me: I know, babydoll Black Ken lol.

Him: Hey, my honey bee.

Me: Buzzing all around your bush.

Him: I can feel it.

Me: I can too.

Him: Lots of energy.

Me: Ooh mi gusta! I feel all of you, darling. I'm going to whisper in your ear, "Mi gusta…mi gusto Papi."

Him: Okay and I'm gonna act like I know what it means.

Me: It means "It pleases me…it pleases me, Daddy."

Him: Aye! Home sweet home?

Me: Yes, sir. I'm just resting this body before I go to the gym.

Him: Yes…rest that body, baby. Brick house…

Me: I don't know about a brick…maybe a playhouse. It'll be sweat everywhere.

Him: Give me a kiss.

Me: I'll kiss you back.

Him: Two more days.

Me: Yep. I'm gone put my green thumb on you to see if you'll grow.

Him: What seed did you plant?

Me: The one on your soul.

Him: Good answer.

Him: Hey, sweets.

Me: Hey, pudding. How is your morning going?

Him: Pretty good.

Me: Nice. Mine is going well. I've been working hard today.

Him: I can't wait to get these hands on your body and rub you down.

Me: I could use a deep-tissue massage right about now. Reflexology, yoga, all of it.

Him: Yes, I got you, baby.

Me: So how are we going to endure after this weekend? Should I look at it as "The Last Supper"?

Him: Let's just get enough.

Me: Okay.

Him: You're gonna hang late?

Me: Yes, sir.

Him: With me? On Friday?

Me: Yes, I'll be there. I'll be sluggish though. I have to get up early. Will that be an issue?

Him: No it won't be. I thought that you were camping out with me?

Me: I am.

Him: You can sleep in then.

Me: Okay good because I'm going to need it. I've had 7 invitations for this weekend and I declined all except for 1.

Him: Those invites shouldn't matter when this was pre-planned, correct?

Me: I was saying it meaning that none of them mattered except for yours.

Him: Awwww. My honeybee is so sweet.

Me: Hopefully forever.

Him: Yes, baby…long as you act right…lol.

Me: I'll never act right. That's why you like me so much.

Him: Ditto.

Him: I can give you some temporary act right in my room.

Me: If you put my face in the pillow, just don't suffocate me, Papi.

Him: Dig dat.

Me: Let me stop playing with you.

Him: I miss my honeybee.

Me: I sense all of you. I miss you too, Papi.

Him: I'm glad that you do too.

Me: I've missed you since I stepped back from leaving you the last time.

Him: Yeah, me too…I was missing you as I watched you walk away.

Me: One step at a time.

Him: But it also felt good to know what we just shared, so that helped a little.

Me: I will embrace what you're able to give to me (as far as energy exchange).

Him: Me too.

Him: I miss those kisses…hell, I miss everything.

Me: Those caramel kisses with a dab of chocolate.

Him: Mocha.

Him: It feels new every time.

Me: Yes indeed. It's hard to focus on work today.

Him: Why…what's wrong, baby?

Me: I want to do something fun.

Him: Like?

Me: Um…something like walking and resting under a waterfall, going go-cart racing, or playing softball. Yeah…something like that.

Him: It seems like you're always doing something exciting…go for it. You have to keep your mind busy.

Him: Hey, sweet lips.

Me: Hey, my Golden Graham.

Him: How are you this morning?

Him: I'm eagerly awaiting your arrival.

Me: Kiss kiss. I know…I'm right there with you, sugar.

Me: Hey, sweet thang.

Him: Hey, sugar foot.

Me: I need to see a pic of you holding some "blankets" before I step foot through your door…

Him: Huh??? It's too hot for blankets.

Me: I should've said "gloves"

Him: Okay. I'll put them on the screen door and let you bring them in.

Me: Lol nope, I want to see a pic of you holding those lil suckers in your hands.

Him: Okay…I'm at work right now. How is your day going?

Me: Okay, I'll wait until you get off. You'll have time before I head your way. My day is going good. How are you making it through?

Him: BARELY!!!

Me: My poor friend…I don't like that at all.

Him: I love our talks.

Me: Thank you, Golden Graham. I send him a quote that I found that said, "Did you know alcohol removes stress, worries, a bra, panties, and boxers?"

Him: Yes…ohhh so well.

Me: I'm about to head home. I'll update you soon on when I'm heading your way. But first, where is my pic of you holding up the gloves? I'll be leaving at 6:30 p.m.

Him: How are you baby?

Me: I'm good, just getting some things in order for next Saturday. How are you?

Him: I'm good…just preparing for this workweek. I wish that you would've left a scent of yourself that I can smell when I'm missing you.

Me: Thanks for the compliment.

Him: You're welcome. Or…I could just smell my upper lip.

Me: For what?! It won't smell like nothing!

Him: It smells like rain.

Me: You miss me?

Him: Yes…like crazy.

Me: I can feel it. I'm in the same space.

Him: I didn't get enough.

Me: I keep thinking about resting on you.

Him: I know right. You sure wasn't shy about it.

Me: Resting on your back.

Him: Oh…I thought that you meant when you squatted.

Me: You are the "Grier" to my "Nola." I'm sure that you don't know what that means, but I'm sure you will do your research. I'll give you a hint: "She's Got to Have It."

Him: Yes, I know all about Nola Darling. I know…Toni Darling.

Him: That's your type of stuff there.

Me: Yeah, you like me just the way that I am.

Him: Yep. "Seductresa."

Me: Kiss kiss.

Him: Hey, baby.

Me: I think that someone likes me...a lot. How is your day going? Any plans for the week?

Him: You think? It's going good. No plans, baby...just getting in that yard.

Me: Am I wrong? I think that I'm right, but I could be wrong lol. My emotions and feelings can be off balance...but I'm not sure.

Him: Have our energy and vibes ever failed us yet?

Him: Miss you.

Me: I miss my "Grier" too.

Him: Do you, darling?

Me: Absolutely. Has anyone ever compared you to him before?

Him: Nope, I've never been compared to Grier.

Me: Especially the fact that you said that you were willing to check out some galleries with me and how you brag on how good you are in bed.

Him: Huh?! I don't brag.

Me: Yeah you do...remember that hula-hoop noise that you always make?!

Him: You like that hula-hoop, why you're talking.

Me: I just instantly smiled because I can hear you making the sounds and doing the movements now.

Him: Hahaha! You like it...every time.

Him: Yummy yummy lol.

Him: I got cheated out of my time with you.

Me: I don't think that things were in alignment with us. There were a lot of roadblocks this weekend. You want a redo, don't you?

Him: Yes I do. I need a whole weekend. Maybe we can even take a trip.

Me: Oh…a whole one?

Him: Yes…a whole one.

Me: Friday morning–Sun evening or Friday evening–Sun morning?

Him: Friday afternoon until Sun evening.

Me: Well all right, that's been stamped with a certified envelope. I'll see what I can do about that.

Him: But until then I need to see you ASAP.

Me: I know. I'm waiting on you to hit the trail with me on these weekdays.

Him: Yes. I thought you were busy every weekend?

Me: I said weekdays…you are not slick.

Him: A mess. I wasn't trying to be slick, baby.

Me: Well, I'm waiting on you.

Him: Oh okay, I'll be on board next week, baby. Word is bond.

Me: Okay, I'm holding you to it. Come even if it rains. I have umbrella available for you.

Him: Oh really. I can dance under water and not get wet.

Me: Yes. I need your hugs. I'm talking about real umbrellas by the way, not "gloves."

Him: Oh okay.

Me: Nasty. Don't temp me.

Him: 'Cause you'll sit right down on a grill.

Me: There will be a sizzle and the juices will fall right on the hot coal. Juices all through the grill. A backyard BBQ.

Him: Couch potato grill.

Me: You are crazy. That's why I like you so much. You make my day.

Him: Ditto, baby. We help each other's day pass swiftly.

Me: Who knew that it would be you? Who knew that it would be me?

Him: I know, right. Honestly…I kinda did…because I get what I want.

Me: Confident and hella cocky. I don't mind it. You only got a glimpse of me. You haven't walked into my paradise yet.

Him: There's levels to this shit.

Me: Exactly. My eyes will stay slanted on the "Cat Eye."

Him: Yeah, I know…until you climax, then all bets are off. You'll need a "Snickers" bar.

Me: My longevity game is quite strong and wondrous. I'm not sure about that.

Him: You are not yourself when you climax. "When you're not yourself…have a Snickers."

Me: Oh yeah I know. Snickers are my favorite candy. Even the look of Snickers turns me on. It looks like a throbbing vein in a "bone." Especially the "fun" size.

Him: Yes absolutely.

Me: Okay, I'm done now.

Him: Tapped out.

Him: How was your walk?

Me: I've been dancing around my place and cleaning instead. I'm still burning calories.

Him: Oh okay. "Get it get it. Dance…too much booty in the pants."

Me: Lol thank you. I've gotta keep this body limber at all times. You know?

Him: Good morning, Queen.

Me: Grand rising, Emperor. Did you see how orange the sun looked this morning?

Him: Yes, it's still bright as hell now. How are you feeling this morning?

Me: It's so beautiful! I was able to see it rise this morning.

Him: Oh wow…great.

Me: How was your sleep last night? Did you get your test results back?

Him: I'll get them back this week. My sleep was off and on.

Me: Have you been on any other dates lately.

Him: No, not at all baby. Slim pickings.

Me: It's so crazy because men have so many to pick from. Or…women (like me) have so many men to choose from, yet we're so selective. I feel sorry for people who have no options.

Him: That's me…I have no options.

Me: Stop playing. I see differently. What makes you say that?

Him: Huh? What could you possibly see, baby?

Me: I see women showing that they're interested in you. Why do you say you have no options? Not every woman that you come across is "dry" or "married." I'm sure that there are some good single women for you to choose from. Not from a relationship standpoint, but to chill, entertain, and travel with.

Him: I'm picky, baby.

Me: Explain, sweetie.

Him: I don't just jump for a smile and moist snatch. I like what I like.

Me: I get that part. Is it all connection and vibes or other things?

Him: All connections and vibes…and I can't stand materialistic-shallow women.

Me: I see. I think that I know why you're attracted to me so much.

Him: Oh really?

Me: Yep. So how do you handle all of those women lusting for you?

Him: I remain a gentleman and I just counteract the majority of them with mere spinoff gestures.

Me: Oh…okay. Did they address the spins? Do you have women prepare meals for you?

Him: No…I cook for myself, baby. They don't address the spins unless they "know me know me"…like go way back…then they talk their slick shit.

Me: Ohhh okay. If you ever want me to leave you alone, just simply tell me. No spinoffs please and thanks.

Him: I'm the same way, baby.

Me: Okay. I tried to walk away in the beginning, but you didn't want me to.

Him: …and when I say spinoff, I don't mean games or nothing…I just mean an easy letdown.

Me: I understand. I'm about to head out and I don't like texting and driving. I'll let you relax because I know you leave soon.

Him: All right, baby, we'll catch up later on. I almost feel sleepy…not sure if it's boredom or just didn't get enough sleep last night.

Me: It's probably because you have a lot of energies coming at you all at once through your calls, texts, and people trying to holler at you. I'm sure that's what's causing it.

Him: Cut it out.

Me: I'm just telling the truth…you know it. It tires me out too. That's how I know.

Him: I just didn't sleep good.

Me: Sure.

Him: …since you got all the answers.

Him: Baby, you've been quiet today. Why haven't I heard from you? Is everything all right?

Me: I was in a meeting. I'm going to call you back in a few. One of my friends is venting to me right now.

Him: I'm just now leaving work, baby, call me back. He sends me a quote that says, "I hate going to the kitchen and finding out I'm the only snack in the house."

Me: Whatever lol. I guess that she wanted a snack too.

Him: You do too.

Me: I'on know about that one.

Him: Oh…so you're acting brand new?

Me: I'm only acting off the energy that is given. It's a reflection. I thought that you had to take a nap? I send him a quote that reads, "Him: I love you. Her: Okay, do them hoes know that?"

Him: You are a mess. I'm just lying here (in the dark). My fault, baby...I was lining things up with my family for tomorrow. They were going to link up with me to hang out.

Me: I have to mess with you at least once a week. If I don't jolt you every now and then, I'm not doing my job. I have some plans for tomorrow as well. I will be meeting about 5 friends for a party. I'm sure that I'll run into more. I know that the DJ is going to play all our favorite songs.

Him: Btw...you and I may have to reschedule for the next time we meet. It wasn't properly planned on my behalf. If you wanna cut me off over that so be it.

Me: Okay.

Him: I totally understand what "okay" means on your end. I know it's mainly out of disappointment, baby. I can feel your energy right now. I didn't really think this visit all the way through. Our chemistry is way too strong for you to diss me like this though...especially when I'm in the business of making things up when I drop the ball.

Me: I'm upset. I don't really want to discuss it right now. More so disappointed. I prepared myself for it though.

Him: In my head, I was creating ways to make this up. It's my turn to make it right. We can't keep this hurting energy going. I'm trying to give you time to forgive me, baby. Meet me at the beach for the sunset, blankets, and pillows.

Me: That's my kind of vibe.

Him: That's where I'm at now. I know it's your kind of vibe, baby.

Me: Nice.

Him: You're giving me a dry vibe, baby...don't do me like this.

Me: Go figure.

Him: I'm almost sure that you had an amazing night without me hanging with your friends. You probably didn't think about me one time.

Me: I'm just sitting here and having an amazing time. It doesn't take much.

Him: I know…especially all depending on what you're sitting on.

Me: I'm not sitting on nothing that melts.

Him: I'm sure.

Me: Get some rest. I know that you haven't slept well.

Him: How did you know? It's been miserable.

Me: Someone told me last night that they could see that I'm "Classy Nasty" (whatever that means). I can feel your energy. You aren't as happy there when I'm not around.

Him: Very true. Yes…you are Classy Nasty.

Me: I tried to uplift your spirits.

Him: Uplift this man.

Me: I put the "holy oil" on you already. Now go and be well lol.

Him: Only way that you win with me is if you sit on my face.

Me: Nope…I'm retired from everybody. I'm delivered!!

Him: I'm in your head and your heart already.

Me: Nope…read that message again. Then repeat.

Him: Yep. I need to see you.

He sends me some motivational quotes on health.

Me: So are you telling me that you're eating clean today? I'm proud of you. You're still on punishment though.

Him: Okay…that's fine. I guess that I'll entertain myself.

Me: You have a whole litter of pussy…quit playing.

Him: How are you seeing what I can't see?

Me: I have special powers that you can't see.

Him: I have no litter.

Me: Okay.

Him: I hope that you had an amazing time last night.

Me: Yeah it was nice, yet a little awkward. Overall I enjoyed myself though.

Him: Why was it awkward?? …ran into a lot of skeletons?

Me: No, not a lot. Just one in particular (the one that I told you about). He made me uncomfortable. He called me the Devil and he was drunk.

Him: Wow.

Me: I ended up slapping him.

Him: Bad girl. I bet slapping him turned you on.

Me: He just laughed and he called me this morning, so I'm guessing that it turned him on.

Him: I said that it turned you on.

Me: No. No turn on for me.

Him: You know that you're strange like that.

Me: I've never hit you, have I?

Him: Come to think about it, you've never raised your hand to me or thrown an object at me. I must be a special person in your life.

Me: Can I?

Him: But you have been slacking on us. You know where I'm at.

Me: Okay. I'll keep that in mind.

Him: I miss you and our energy. I know that you have a "fan club."

Me: I'm about to hibernate, man. I can't win. You just don't know. I've only spent quality time with you in the last few months. I've noticed a change in myself. To be honest, I don't give a fuck about men for real.

Him: Oh really.

Me: I'm serious.

Him: Obviously. Why the man hate?

Me: It's a long story. If you've been shitted on as much as I have, you would have the same heart too. But anyways, I don't want to be an ass, so I'll just stop there and let you enjoy your day.

Him: Okay, baby. You're still my baby, right…or naw??

Me: I don't know. I'm running from my feelings so that you can't hurt me too.

Him: Oh wow…if anyone does the hurting it will be you.

Me: I used to be sweet as pie at one point. Men don't like sweet pie. They like them tart.

He sends me a song by David Ruffin called "Walking Away from Love."

Me: That's what you're about to do too? Walk away from love?

Him: No…that was toward you for you. It was your reasons for falling back on me.

Me: How can love be walked away from if it wasn't present to begin with?

Him: Just listen to the lyrics, stubborn woman. You're on one today. You are not your typical self today. I wonder why?

Me: I told you that I was always nice to you. Do you believe me now? Since I can't have my way with you how I want it, I'm converting back to how I was before we met.

Him: Oh wow. What way was that, baby? I'm right here…I never left or fell back.

Me: I can't physically touch you when I want. I'm spoiled. I need my way. Yes…it's a need and not a want.

Him: I can't touch you either, baby, so how do think that I feel? You know that I like gripping that ass and kissing every inch of you.

Me: You're not doing anything about it, which is why I've been upset with you lately.

Him: You don't know what I'm doing, baby…on Saturday I made plans to come see you during the week. But…your energy changed so I didn't really know what to do. You ain't gotta put up no front for me, baby…I know what you like and how you like it.

Me: I'm still waiting to see your results from your test. I need to make sure that we're having a clean partnership. Even though we've gone through this process before, I want you to have an updated screening. I like to be fully free.

Him: I'm actually going today…I was able to push my date up.

Me: I'm glad that you're going and taking your health seriously.

Him: I'm telling real stories…based on real people.

Me: You should become an author then.

Him: I been an author. I wrote all in your insides. Tell the story, baby.

Me: I'll have to check out some of your works. Somehow amnesia must've settled in. Perhaps you'll have to run the story by me once more.

He sends me the address to his house.

Me: Is that the location for the storytelling?

Him: Yes…and story writing.

Me: Oh okay, I'll try to store it in the memory this time around.

He sends me the results for his STD tests. They all come back negative.

Me: Yes!! Thanks for sharing this pertinent information with me.

Him: No doubt. All you have to do is learn some patience, baby. I told you that I was good.

Me: I know. I'm getting better. I was way worse and mean before.

Him: Good.

Him: You never sent my picture that you promised me.

Me: That's because I didn't take one.

Him: Smartass. You miss this dick.

Me: Why thank you, sir, for calling me smart. I think the same about myself.

Him: I'll make sure to punish that ass.

Me: I'm just listening to soft rock, enjoying breakfast, and minding my own business. That's it.

Him: Same here, boo.

He sends me a quote: Every girl's #1 weakness is black cock.

Me: Black cock is not my weakness. Wordplay is my weakness. I'm a sapiosexual. I fall in love with intelligence. Intelligence is what keeps me wet during the day and helps me sleep at night.

Him: Yeah, I know.

He sends me a birthday message: Happy Birthday, Queen...may your Rain/Reign continue forever.

Me: My Sweet Emperor...thank you so much!! I'll keep it wet and reign as much as I can.

Him: Are we still on for Saturday? I miss you, baby. I'll cook for you, wash your back, give you a deep-tissue massage, and stimulate every inch of your body from head to toe. I need you.

Me: I'll try to come over, but I'm not sure.

Him: I need to feel you...touch you, taste you, wine you, dine you, and double-time you.

Me: You are something else, man.

Him: Do you feel my energy?

Me: Yes I do. I know that you need me right now. I'm leaning more toward yes. It will be okay. I'll rub on your head and shoulders soon.

Him: That's why you're my baby. T Rain in that thang.

Me: Haha! Stop it please.

Him: What are you doing? I need facial expressions.

Me: What kind of expressions?

Him: Seeing your face, Queen.

Him: My Dr. said something about reflexology twice a month and some couch love…whatever that means.

Me: Okay…now that was hilarious.

Him: Oh yeah…so basically he said that I needed to work out more.

Me: You don't look heavy at all to me, which is bizarre. But Drs. know best…most times. Sexology and walking are the quickest ways to drop weight fast.

Him: Yeah I know. I remember reading something about that.

Him: We can walk the trail in the park of your choice…but no panties are allowed at the park. I don't know why they say that.

Me: I cannot stand you today. You are seriously making all this up. I'm quite sure that there is not one sign that reads that. "Why are you picking with me, baby?" As you would say.

Him: 'Cause you like to be picked with.

Me: Just don't pick with my heartstrings. That's all I ask.

Him: I won't. How could I possibly do that to a strong woman such as yourself?

Me: Women of color are the most hated and most disrespected on earth. I'll never understand it.

Him: I was saying as far as you allowing it.

Me: You're right.

I finally give in to meet with him.

Him: Have you gotten enough of me?

Me: No, but I won't become overbearing…I promise.

Him: Stay hungry. The inner fire that burns for me won't go out.

Me: How are you so certain? If you make it past 3 years, then you're cold work.

Him: Freeze then.

Me: I'm not talking about just summers either.

Him: Me either.

Me: You need to quit playing and come eat this…never mind.

Him: We are overdue.

Me: So what's the 411 with "old girl" that you said that you were dating at one point?

Him: Not really sure…don't care…haven't spoken in so long that she doesn't even matter anymore at this point. I'm trying to focus on you and only you.

Me: I had a feeling that something was up because you're always available for me. I appreciate you being open with me about it.

Him: I was always available for you anyway.

Me: I remember you saying that you wouldn't always be available on the weekends. Now you're always available.

Him: Yep…always. I told you that my world revolves around you now.

Me: I see…you did say that, Emperor. But…I'll have to admit that you're a distraction for me right now. I have to get ready for a meeting.

Him: Okay, get nice and pretty. Think about me and play with that pussy under the table.

Me: Would you stop?!

Him: Oh yeah…my fault. Do something to make me feel good.

I send him a quote: I'm not riding dick for more than 5 mins. You knew I was fat before you came over.

Him: You'll ride a face though. Indeed...25 mins.

Me: Huh?

Him: That's how long you'll ride a face.

Me: How do you know?

Him: Lucky guess.

Him: How are you this morning?

Me: Better now that I've got some laughs in with you. I've been so overwhelmingly busy.

Him: Stay focused, baby...I'm in your corner.

Me: Thank you, sugar. I feel like a one-person army sometimes.

Him: It does seem like that at times...but it makes for a better and confident outcome.

Me: You're right. I will try to keep that as a reminder.

Him: No doubt, baby...I'm your biggest fan.

Me: You're trying to make me smile. It's working.

Him: I'm serious...just stay focused. I won't distract you either.

Me: Yeah you will.

Him: I promise. Your cup always seems full and you're always full of energy and power. I am your priority...you better recognize, wicked one.

Me: No you're not, sir. You don't wanna be saved!

Him: I'm missing you, baby. You're fighting the fact that you're missing me, but you'd rather be stubborn and a savage. I don't care what side everyone else sees. I know it's not you.

Me: What's my side?

Him: The side that we click on.

Me: That side scares me.

Him: I don't see how.

Me: It's not the right timing for me to be falling in love with anyone right now.

Him: That's the fun part…because you're dealing with a real one.

Me: That's not fun for the soul.

Him: Who are you trying to convince…me or yourself?

Me: Convince of what exactly?

Him: The fact that you don't miss me and that you're falling in love…

Cake

I stick my fork into you and pick up just enough to fit in my mouth.

The first bite is uniquely flavored.

Your taste is distinct, like the other layers of you.

I want more.

This sweet texture on my taste buds with a drizzle of buttercream.

The filling of this cake is the cream of the crop.

You're mesmerized by the thought and sight of me tasting you.

I think that you want to smash a piece of it in my face.

I want you to.

I think that I want another piece.

I then ask for a bigger and thicker one.

You cut it just the size that I ask for…you make it bigger.

Now I'm full.

It's the best cake that I've ever had.

Tea Time

Me: I'd like for us to enjoy some sips of tea. I'll let you know when it's ready to be served.

Him: I'll drink straight from the pot until the tea overflows from the temperature rising. Then I'll stick my spoon in to stir up the honey. Lemme know if you want me to add cream. Are you at work?

Me: Make sure that you tap the bottom of that pot that you're drinking from...I don't want not one drop to go to waste. Yes...I'm working today.

Him: Oooh you know what I wanna see when you at work.

Me: Stop it. There's too many around right now.

Him: It's more fun to sneak when people are around. Bring pretty kitty out of hiding.

Me: I want to be good so bad. You are not going to stop until you get what you want, huh?

Him: I bet she's wet right now thinking about my kisses, isn't she? Touch her for me.

Me: I cannot concentrate and you know that my poker face is trash. Quit it.

Him: Well...spread those thighs and slide that dress up some. Think of me under your desk.

Me: You are going on punishment until next week. You're acting up.

Him: I'd have you moaning so loud…squeezing your thighs around my head as you drip and squirt. I wanna taste Ms. Kitty from the back until you run.

Me: You think that you're so funny, right? I'm going to get you for doing this to me.

Him: I want you to send me some pics. Matter of fact, you're gonna not only send me some, but you're going to take some just for me too. Did you touch her yet for me?

Me: Just when I thought that you were done acting up… I'm trying to stop smiling. Seriously.

Him: Touch her for me since I ain't there to kiss her. Taste her and let me know how sweet she is…smile hard as you do it. You wearing a dress?

Me: I am, sir.

Him: You wearing panties?

Me: Would you stop?

Him: But we still gotta finish our session. We've only had a half of one because we were interrupted.

Me: I'm not being myself right now in this moment. I feel like I'm floating and elevating in my seat right now.

Him: I had Ms. Kitty send me a big wet kiss, huh? You got the juice? Is Ms. Kitty gonna grab me back?

Me: You are trying to trap me.

Him: Lemme see her so I can start my day off on a good note. Do you have coffee cake for me to go with my tea?

Instrument

Sit on both of your knees leaning against the edge of the bed.

Your eyes looking straight ahead.

I see you.

I'm asked to scoot down just a bit more.

One foot is gripped by your hand…then the other.

Your fingers then move around each ankle.

I'm not there yet.

My legs are pulled down, drawn closer to you.

I've glided…right in front of you.

One leg is now ready.

The other leg follows the leader.

A warm forehead is now a shadow over my "Love Pillow."

I feel a blow.

It's soft and low.

A whirl of wind is twirling over my small peak.

A chin is then tucked nestled over the top of my cheeks.

Your lips are now in a position as if playing my flute.

I feel another blow, followed by simultaneous blows… and then a kiss.

Once I'm there, all the sheets are gripped, then I'm dripped all
into you.

Go on, boy… play that flute.

Nothing matters on the outside if the insides of you aren't loving, sincere, and pure. You can wear the coverings to make yourself look "good," but in the end, none of that even matters.

Mesmerized

Him: So are you gonna come see me?

Me: Why of course. I've got some things to take care of today, but I'm gonna get up there my usual time.

Him: Okay. Well, I'll see you then. I love your style and the way that you dress.

Me: You're so sweet and humorous. I love being around you. See you soon.

Him: All that sexy material that you wear have me feeling some type of way. See you soon.

Me: It has you feeling some type of way? Well, maybe I'll have to put you on a different track then. I'll see you, silly man.

Him: Lmao. I love it.

Me: *Wink* I thought that you would.

Him: I'm a good guy, but you know my mind is in the gutter right now.

Me: Yeah I caught that. Sometimes you can't help how you really feel.

Him: You're right about that. I just don't want to ruffle no feathers. But...you have the juice.

Me: I'll make sure the feathers are put in place. I'm not easily blown over, so you're good. You've done well in the past with not giving me too much wind.

Him: True, but you do know that there's usually a calm before the storm, right? Well, I think the storm is coming and it's a hurricane!! Lol I'm just kidding. Let me slow down.

Me: Oh…so you think that you have that type of might to make natural disasters happen, huh? Well, they say it's a first for everything, but I don't think it applies to all.

Him: I have the DNA makeup to actually move mountains! Your energy is amazing woman. You better stop because once I pop, the fun don't stop.

Me: That may be true, but I'm known to cause artesian wells to form…they're very beautiful when one sees them explode. Watch your words because sometimes you may speak things into existence.

Him: My body armor is built for any type of weather that is ahead of me. I believe I can walk through it and come out on the other end with a smile. I might even want to run right back into it if it was really real and not a dream.

Me: So you like feeling like a kid again?? You like running through water and jumping in puddles? See…I too have a strong mental capacity as you. Let's not run on water. Someone can slip and fall and bump their head. You know?

Him: Yeah, you're right. But…water is the key to life. If the water won't stop running, I guess that I'll have to stay after work hours until it stops…I'm a handy man.

Me: I see. I see. You do have a point there, young man. Too much of anything can be too much. Sometimes it can cause some confusion.

Him: You're so right about that. Confusion only happens when you're confused…a strong mind can handle it. If the task at hand is overwhelming, then I understand.

Me: Hmmm. I wasn't expecting this convo to be on my agenda for today. So much for a relaxed Friday. We'll just let things play out how they've always been…for now.

Him: Will do.

Me: I can't stand you for real.

Him: Yes you can…more than you know.

Me: I'm also a runner. I'm good at dodging bullets.

Him: I don't shoot bullets. I drop bombs, Ma. You can't run too far from those.

Me: More than likely I'll explode if I can't run from those. I'll have to be very cautious of my moves from now on.

Him: Yes you will. This is chess…not checkers.

Me: I thought so. I don't know how to play chess though, so I'm sure I'll fail. I might as well get out the game now.

Him: It's your call. Can I share something with you?

Me: I'll keep that in mind. What would you like to share?

I receive a dick pic.

Him: This is my current situation.

Me: Wowsers! I thought it was something in writing, but now I see it's something graphical. You look healthy I must say.

Him: Watch out now.

Me: You are so vicious.

Him: Lol I just wanted to ease your mind a little.

Me: No, you just wanted to give me a little incentive push to help with my decision-making.

Him: Good catch.

Me: Yep, with both hands and the chin.

Him: All over, huh? Don't duck.

Me: I have to…I don't wanna get tagged.

Him: After I tag you, then it's your turn.

Me: You are gonna get out of breath trying to get me. I don't get a turn.

Him: I'm good with angles…you will get a turn.

Me: Oh goodness. You are gonna be a lot of work I see.

Him: Mhmm.

Me: Poor me. My antennas are still up with you. You're not as slick as you think you are.

Him: I'm not going to try to be slick anymore. That was a nice way of you telling me no.

Me: You know that I had to say no anyways. You're a smart guy.

Him: The talk was very fun though.

Me: Thanks. Everything that I do is an adventure. Enjoy your weekend.

Him: Lol. Thanks and you enjoy yours as well.

Me: I appreciate you.

Him: Likewise.

We meet up on a Monday after the weekend.

Me: Thanks for showing up and spending time with me today.

Him: You know that I was going to come and see that smile.

Me: Watch out now. *wink*

Him: Lol you are too funny.

A few days go by and we plan to go to an arcade later in the week.

Him: Good morning.

Me: Good morning to you as well. What time should I be expecting you?

Him: I don't want to tell a lie. It's better if I don't say a time, but I will definitely be there. You know how you are so punctual when it comes to time.

Me: Yes indeed. I'm not a night person, so I won't be waiting too long. I know you're a busy person.

Him: I'm not going to make you wait.

Me: Good. We don't want you to be on punishment, now, do we?

Him: Maybe punishment is not so bad.

Me: Yeah, sometimes punishments can turn into a joyful bliss.

Him: There you go.

He actually shows up again and we have a great time.

Me: Good morning and thanks for showing up and being very punctual yesterday. I had a good time with you once again. I hope that you enjoyed yourself also.

Him: Good morning to you. I had fun and thank you for showing up as well.

He sends me a picture of his face.

Me: You better stop playing with me.

Him: What did I do now?

Me: You know what you are doing.

Him: No I don't.

Me: Your eyes tell everything…just like mine. I'm not going to get blown away though.

Him: You keep saying that….just don't eat your words.

Me: Oh I won't have to. I have a light appetite.

Him: Okay I hear you.

Him: Mhmm.

Me: You ain't that cute anyways lol.

Days later we discuss our feelings on dominance.

Him: Nope. Nope. You won't be beating me up and shit…butt-ass naked.

Me: Haaaa!!! It's not about being beaten. It's a misconception that people have. I've never beat anyone. I've been a "Good Girl" as of late. My path has been clean, but I may want to get a little dirty soon.

Him: I do want to learn more about your potential though.

Me: You would be surprised that people find pleasure in being told what to do. I know how to work erogenous areas of the body that a lot of people don't know about or pay attention to. That is the major reason why they ALWAYS come back to me.

Him: That's crazy.

Me: Mhmm.

Him: You miss it?

Me: Honestly…yes.

Him: I can tell that you do.

Me: I think that you have a little curiosity. Now you watch out before I come tug on your shirt.

Him: Wow! You are so funny.

Me: I be enticing people on accident.

Him: Right. I believe you. It's crazy.

Me: Yeah it is.

Him: It's a skill.

Me: Yeah you're right. People think that just because you're pretty/handsome, that they can pull people. It's definitely not the case.

Him: It's sex appeal that gets them.

Me: Absolutely. It's also the energy that you give off. I hope that I have mine forever. I want to maintain my sex appeal until I'm a "seasoned" woman.

Him: You will if you stay doing what you're doing.

Me: Yes, sir. I have to keep it going, glowing, and flowing.

Him: What? The juices??

Me: Why you ask? You want me to squeeze some in your cup?

Him: Hahaha! I'm just kidding.

Me: Don't be shy.

Him: You are hilarious.

Me: I'm only teasing you for real.

Him: I know. Are you trying to bring out your alter ego again?

Me: My costumes are hanging up, but they will be brought out when you're ready.

Him: What do they look like?

Me: You'll just have to see. What's your favorite color?

Him: Navy blue.

Me: Or what color would you like to see?

Him: Red.

Me: Oh okay. So you want a treat? You want to play in one of my skits?

Him: Like how though?

Me: You nervous?

Him: Yes.

Me: Good. I want you to shiver.

Him: Why?

Me: I can't tell all my secrets.

Him: I see.

Me: I think that you know that you may like it too much…which is why you're nervous.

Him: What type of things though.

Me: Which of your body parts do you like fondled with most?

Him: My dick. Do you like your ass to be played with?

Me: Don't you worry about that.

Him: Yeah you do. Nothing wrong with it.

Me: I'm "pleading the 5th" on what I do and enjoy. Can I clamp your nipples one by one?

Him: Ha!! Hell naw!

Me: Hahaha!!

Him: Let me do yours.

Me: You will like it. I promise you will.

Him: No way lol.

Me: Can I clamp the ends of your ass cheeks?

Him: No way. What else you got that's freaky for me?

Me: Can I sit on top of you and pretend that you're a pony? Or will you pretend that you're a lion in jungle looking for his lioness?

Him: Maybe.

Me: I'm sad again. I'm about to go and take a shower. I'll cry while I'm in there. Hopefully my pain will go away.

Him: Why are you sad?

Me: You don't want to let me have my way. You don't wanna play.

Him: You are a bad girl. I want to play dirty.

Me: We will see, huh? How?

Him: Nipple clamp me. Tie me up.

Me: I knew it!! I knew it!!

Him: What?

Me: I knew that you would like "Pony Play."

Him: Lol! No! What is it?

I send him a few different pictures of Pony Play.

Him: Just keep the whips and chains away.

Me: Who me??! Well…I'll keep the whip and oil in the bag just in case.

Him: No whips. Oil is cool.

Me: Okay.

Him: You are funny. I love it.

Me: Thanks. I love your humor too.

Him: You better watch yourself, young lady.

Me: See, I told you I was going to be good, but you want me to spark my lighter.

Him: Lol okay I'm done.

Me: Don't get bit.

Him: Don't bite.

Me: Would you prefer that I nibble?? Okay. I'm done now.

Him: I will blow your entire mind with just my tongue.

Me: Oh boy! Don't tempt me. Get back, Satan. Haha!

Him: Lol okay I'm done.

Me: No, you're not done until I tell you that it's okay for you to stop.

Him: I'm the type to eat your pussy and would probably never call you back again.

Me: What?! You're getting a whooping for that! If you want, I can pump your brakes for you. Man. You shouldn't have started with me.

Him: How can you do that?

Me: I don't have to use my hands. I'll just say that.

Him: What would you use?

Me: Quit playing with me.

Him: I'm asking.

He sends me a dick pic.

Me: Oh my! What a big fang you have, "Count Dracula."

Him: That's funny!!

Me: I would say that you made my day, but I don't know if that would be appropriate.

Him: It's okay to say it.

Me: Well, you definitely made my day. I didn't know that you were a vampire.

Him: I want to suck your pussy.

Me: Omg! That was fucking hilarious! I'm definitely interested in that. My antennas are up.

Him: Antennas? Oh…so you're interested in that, huh? Are you ready to bring the freak out?

Me: Well, one of the antennas are up. The other one is still trying to find static. I can't put my all into you right now.

Him: Try hard.

Me: I'll try HARDER.

Him: Well, I know that you have some paperwork to take care of. While you do that, I'm about to release some stress.

Me: Thanks for giving me a "puddle" in my underwear. I'm about to handle my business and get some work done. You enjoy your time pleasing yourself.

Him: You better mop that puddle up.

Me: Perhaps I can use your hair to mop and soak up the moisture.

Him: You can.

Me: Okay seriously. I'm done this time.

Him: I want to bust a nut all on those tits while I'm jacking.

Me: Is that so? I'm sure that you'll get lost in this "Treasure Island."

Him: No way. But how does that sound?

Me: It sounds tempting and delicious.

Him: Yes. Yes it does.

Him: Soon.

Me: We'll see, won't we?

Him: Yes we will.

Days go by.

Him: Hey.

Me: Good morning.

Him: How have you been?

Me: I've been great. How about yourself?

Him: I'm good other than some pain that I've been getting. Can you help me out?

Me: How may I assist you?

Him: I've been feeling helpless. I can barely move.

Me: When would you like for me to help you?

Him: Whenever you can. I'd like for you to come by tomorrow if that's possible for you.

Me: I think that would work.

Him: …oh and bring the whips and chains lol. I'll be helpless, remember?

Me: You are one funny man. I'll massage you good. Don't worry.

Him: How about a waist-down massage?

Me: Yeah, as long as I don't hit or run over any roadkill.

Him: "That" will need a massage as well.

Me: See. There you go.

Him: What? Did I say something wrong?

Me: You better be nice to me. No touching, no licking, no tasting. Just me massaging you. That's it!

Him: Lol! I thought from the waist down would be harmless.

Me: I'm not trying to cause any problems.

Him: Ha! Okay a foot rub would be cool.

Me: I'm sure that you have lady friends for "that." I promise you'll live and be okay. The massage that I give might even put you to sleep. You'll be okay either way.

Him: We are gonna see. There still may be a body part that might need more attention than the others though.

Me: The foot is connected to the entire body, so really it'll be like I'm hitting every spot.

Him: Now there you go being funny again. Okay, I will just have on my draws when you get here then.

Me: Oh my! (in my Winnie the Pooh voice) You know…it's been a long time since I've tied someone at the foot and pulled on their monkey tail. Don't tempt me.

Him: You can.

Me: So when I call for you, just be ready for a tongue twister.

Him: No. I'm scared!

Me: I know that you are…and I like to keep it that way.

Him: How would you do this?

Me: I told you that I'll never tell all of my secrets. You were just lucky enough to find out a glimpse of my capabilities. I will whisper in your ear about one thing though. I like to pinch on the nips…only lightly though.

Him: I want to know more.

Me: You're just trying to find out what's going to happen to you so that you won't be as scared. You know I'm going to hurt you in a good way don't you??

Him: Lol! Tell me.

Me: Tell me what you want done.

Him: Everything.

Me: Nope. Tell me in story form.

Him: You tell me.

Me: Boo!! You're playing with me again.

Him: No, I'm new to this.

Me: Are you busy on Tuesday? What won't you tolerate. I need to figure out your body first.

Him: I've never been tied up. Pain, I've never felt. I'm fresh. Give me some ideas.

Me: I don't want to give you ideas so you can use them on someone else.

Him: Trust me. I'm not. I'm going to let you "pop my cherry" as they say lol.

Me: I do know that I want to have access to a bathroom because I will be doing "work" in there. I'm gonna have some tasks for you. I'm telling you now so that you don't get nervous.

Him: I'm already nervous.

Me: Pop your cherry…that sounds delicious. I know that you are. Eventually you'll begin to relax. That's why I need access to a bathroom. It will help with the relaxation process.

Him: From what in the bathroom will actually help me to relax?

Me: I can see with you, it'll have to be a random and spur-of-the-moment type of thing. The planning will only get you worked up. Running water will help you. I will be controlling your hands though, just so that you know.

Him: Will I be naked?

Me: No. Not quite.

Him: What will I have on?

Me: I will LET you keep on your boxers/boxer briefs, your wife beater, and socks. I like boxer briefs best.

Him: What else? What will you have on?

Me: See…you got me wanting to experiment with you today, knowing dang well that I can't. I haven't figured out what I'm going to wear yet. It all depends on the location and time of the day.

Him: Okay. Gotcha.

Me: I just know that you will be pleased with whatever I present to you. Since you said that you want to see me in something red, then red is what it will be. I will show some kind of "fairness."

Him: Give me a description please.

Me: What would you like to see me wear?

Him: Fishnets…nothing underneath. A one-piece.

Me: Okay. I'd have to find a red one-piece. I can no longer fit some of the things that I had.

Him: Well…it doesn't have to be red.

Me: Oh okay. So something like a fishnet bodysuit?

Him: Yeah…with the hole in the middle.

Me: Crotchless, right??

Him: Right…and heels.

Me: Oh I know exactly what you're referring to. I didn't say that you get to touch me though.

Him: …and bring your toys because I might want to stick one in you.

Me: Oh really?! I thought that I was the one having all the fun.

Him: You are, but I can't touch.

Me: No touching in my sessions.

Him: Wow! What if I cum fast?

Me: That's gonna be the hardest part for you…the no touching part. Oh…I'm sure that you'll cum fast.

Him: Will you play with it in my face? But what if I do cum fast??

Me: That's fine. I don't care if you cum fast. You might be able to make yourself cum. I might let you touch yourself too.

Him: Aww hell! You're not going to be touching on my dick? Lol you're just going to tease.

Me: I might even have you on your knees staring at my "lips" and my "tongue" while you listen to my commands. Yes…I will be touching you, but you can't touch me.

Him: See…now you're trying to dog walk me. What's the freakiest thing that you've ever done? Have you ever pissed on someone?

Me: No, I haven't pissed on anyone. I've always wanted to. Will you be my candidate?

Him: Yeah, if you also let me piss on you too.

Me: The freakiest thing that I've ever done was wrong on so many levels, but I had the best orgasms that I've ever had in my life.

We end up linking up.

Him: Thanks for coming.

Me: My pleasure. I hope that you enjoyed yourself.

Him: I did. Did you?

Me: Yes I did.

I go months without communication.

Me: My apologies for not being in touch with you. I've just been going through a lot, so I'm just working on taking care of myself right now. I didn't want to send any uneasy energy your way. How are you?

Him: It's okay. I know that life gets tough sometimes and I'm always here if you just need a listening ear.

Me: Thank you and I appreciate it. You're always looking out for people and I respect you for that.

Him: I'm just doing my job and that's being a friend.

Me: Yes. Always.

Him: Hope all gets well soon.

Me: Thank you. It's getting better by the day.

Him: Prayer changes things.

Me: You are definitely right by those words.

Him: I will send some prayers up for you.

Me: You are such an amazing person.

Him: Stop that, woman.

Me: Lol what did I say wrong? Absolutely the truth.

Him: I'm just a friend. Nothing special about being a good friend, you know. This is our foundation and sometimes it has to show.

Me: Well, that's where you're wrong. There are good friends and there are genuine friends. You're a genuine friend (very rare and precious). But yes we do have to make it more present at certain times in our lives.

Him: Yes we do.

He sends me a wink.

Him: You will always be special to me. I hope that you have an awesome day. Before you get me hot and bothered…

Me: I am now. It's too late for me. You have an awesome day as well.

A few days go by.

Him: Hey beautiful. I miss my friend. I have a new number. Make sure that you save it please.

Me: It's nice to hear from you again. I miss my friend as well. I'll save your new #. We should hang out sometime next week if you're available. I prefer Wednesday or Thursday…you know…midweek.

Him: Okay, we can definitely do that.

Me: All right, cool.

Him: The next time that see you, I'd like to hide under your bed.

Me: So you're asking to be the monster or boogieman that hides under the bed?

Him: Yes. I won't frighten you too bad. I might bite on the tips of your toes if they over it.

Me: You better not bite me too hard. I thought that we were going to work on being "good"??

Him: My thirst may be due to my fast.

Me: You need to fast every day then if that's the case.

Him: I was on a fast for over 30 days. I still haven't been intimate.

Me: Is that right? I don't know how much of that is believable.

Him: I'm serious. See how you do me?

Me: Aww you still care about me though.

Him: I do.

I disappear for almost a year…I tend to run away from my emotions at times. He tries to keep in contact and I don't respond.

Me: Hey, my apologies. I know that I haven't been around. The world can be distracting at times. I've been focusing on me more lately.

Him: Okay, I just wanted to make sure that you were well.

Me: Thank you, friend. I hope that all is well with you also.

Him: I miss you a lot. I hope that you're having an amazing weekend.

Me: I miss my friend too. I miss my friend's hugs and our talks. Thank you!

Him: I want us to link up soon.

Me: Okay, I hope so.

Him: Me too.

Me: You better.

Him: I can never impress you enough.

Me: You know that you always do something special to my soul when you want to.

Him: I'm so humble. I never pay attention to my power. I never take advantage of anyone or anything. I appreciate you.

Me: I know what my capabilities are. I'm cocky for the most part. I know the power that is bestowed upon me.

Him: See…I need to know mine.

We make small talk and say our goodbyes.

Him: Damn I love you, woman.

Me: I love you too, friend.

Him: How is your day going?

Me: You better quit telling me that you love me so much. I'm going to start thinking that you're falling in love with me. My day has been going good and it's been productive. I ate some authentic tacos, which made it even better. How is yours?

Him: Nope. I'm never going to quit telling you how much I love you.

Me: See…now I can't deal with you today. You're trying to have me in my feelings.

Him: Yes you can.

Me: I've been good and PRODUCTIVE, I said. You're trying to make me clear my desk off for you.

Him: I need that. But I'm glad that your day is going good.

Me: Thank you. We'll stick to having tea or coffee. That's enough for me right now. Hopefully it'll be soon.

Him: Whenever you like I'm available. Tea time is great. Desk time is a fantasy.

Me: Have you ever had desk time?

Him: No. Wait…I have. Have you?

Me: Yes.

Him: Love it. Damn…I would love to do that with you.

Me: Don't do this to me. Please don't.

Him: What am I doing? You're not worried or think about me.

Me: The pressure. The madness. Let me get back to work.

Him: I don't pressure. You have forgotten all about me.

Me: Never. I've just learned to re-channel that energy elsewhere.

He sends me a few pictures of himself.

Me: You are so damn foul. God dammit you sexy motherfucker you!

Him: Exercise has been working for me.

Me: That "tip" though…my goodness.

Him: Stop that lol. Give me a few more months.

Me: I'm about to…man…I'm about to get back to work. I'm going to catch up with you later.

Him: Wait…I wasn't done talking. But…okay.

We meet up some weeks later.

Him: I have to stop looking at you in a sexual way though, but it's so hard. I be wanting to eat you alive.

Me: Okay sorry. Yeah, you have to change your way of thinking.

Him: Why is it hard to change it for me? I'm strongly attracted to you.

Me: I feel it. I knew that it was going to be trouble when I first saw you. I predicted our friendship.

Him: Yeah, that's so funny. I remember you telling me that. Good times we've had.

Me: Yes…not one bad moment. A few misunderstandings, but never arguments.

Him: Right. Okay…I'm done bugging you for the day. You're making me horny. This is crazy what you do to me.

Me: No I'm not. Well…you might be right. I do know how to tap into your mind like no other. It's probably the massages that you miss.

Him: I do. You got me?

Me: Always.

Him: I'm serious. Full body?

Me: Yes. Promise.

I meet up with him to give a full-body massage.

Me: Thanks for sharing yourself with me.

Him: Just know that I miss you more than you know.

Me: You got my heart fluttering, man. I miss you more.

Him: No way.

Me: Way.

Him: I want to see you again soon.

Me: You better. You make my day brighter.

Him: I will always and forever keep doing my part to raise your vibration.

Me: You do a damn good job at it.

Him: You know that I got you. But…you can't put me in a candy shop and then tell me that I can't eat candy.

Me: That'll be the safest route for us. You can't have sweets all the time.

Him: I'm the good guy.

Me: Not when I tap into you…then you won't be good. You'll be tarnished and scorned.

Him: You're not going to tap into me.

Days go by and he sends me a few pictures of himself…full body.

Me: Boy!! You're just too much for me on a rainy day. You look like a sexy "Chip n Dale Rescue Ranger." You're too motherfucking fine, man.

Him: I'm just trying to get my body right.

Me: You're shaved and oiled down there too? My gawd!!

Him: Yes, fresh out of the shower.

Me: You're so damn bad and I love every bit of it. You're winning and I don't care who says different.

Him: You're so sweet to me.

Me: Thank you for the morning greeting.

Him: Thank you for your inspiration.

Me: You're welcome. Everything is checking out.

Him: Is that right? Now, I'm sexually destroying most of you in my thoughts.

Me: Thine eyes have seen a glimpse of glory this morning.

Him: Don't leave it all up to me.

Me: You claim to be the aggressor, then you tell me what you want from a woman.

Him: I bet that you're not ready for me to eat your pussy. I want you to sit on my face…right now.

Me: Omg! When I call you, you better be ready for me too.

Him: I will.

Me: Your energy is so strong right now.

Him: Can you feel me?

Me: Yes I can. It's the season. It's much stronger in the fall.

Him: Yes indeed.

Days later.

Him: Hey babe. Sex in my office?

Me: You can't pull that off.

Him: Shit…yes I can. I will hit you up in a few hours.

Me: I'm not trying to go to jail for you.

Him: Hahaha! You talk so much shit and now you're scared.

A few days go by. I get some really sweet voice messages. I return his phone call.

Me: You are one the sweetest and most gentle guys that I've ever met. I feel your energy all the time and that's more than enough connection that'll last me a lifetime.

Him: You're so sweet! Thank you so much! We all have it in us. We just are afraid to let the light shine.

Me: I never thought of it that way. Keep speaking the good news, brethren.

Him: I can't change a soul, but I know that I can bring awareness to the conscious of the higher-vibrational beings who are seeking what I have to offer.

Me: You got that right. Most importantly you are a melanated male. That speaks volumes in itself. Prove to them that we can withstand anything.

Him: See, I don't have to prove that to them because they already know that. What I have to do is far beyond color. I'm reaching for the soul, which has no color. I'm going to make them see from a colorblind standpoint.

Me: I hear you! Just know that I'm clapping for you. I support you, sir.

Him: Thank you very much. You're one of the sweetest souls that any friend could ever ask for. I hear your thoughts. We are past the verbal stage in our lives. We have always been past that since the first time we saw each other.

Me: I'm about to run now.

Him: How do you feel? Are you conflicted? Your season is ahead of you.

Me: Like jello lol.

Him: Damn…that boy good!

Me: My limbs are loose.

Him: That's funny. You're caught in the web, babe. Now I can smile. You won my heart.

Me: I'm sure that you tell that to all the "tenderonies" out here.

Him: You know better than to think that.

Me: I haven't teased you in a while. I couldn't miss my opportunity.

Him: Uh huh…yeah I hear you. Where is the bad at? I haven't seen it in a while.

Me: I'm good at being good and I'm good at being bad. I can live in both worlds when I'm focused.

Him: Has your alter ego had a chance to play?

Me: I've had invites, but I've declined them.

Him: So you pulled out the ropes and chains? Damn.

Me: They get addicted because there's not many like me.

Him: Wait…wait. They?? So you're keeping me out of the loop? I'm listening.

Me: It's a "secret society."

Him: Nope. You know that we're locked. I'm trying to figure out how I haven't been let in on this action.

Me: You kicked me to the curb, remember? Lol!

Him: Never. Now you know that's a lie. I would never do that. I gave you your wings and you never flew back.

Me: When was the last time that we even talked?

Him: Uh…like two days ago.

Me: Ha! I'm just messing with you friend.

Him: I'm still your soulmate. I don't care what you say. I'm not tripping. I got a piece of you that they will never have.

Me: Yep…you're right. We're still connected to the soul regardless. I stopped what I was doing to communicate with you right now. See…I just put you first.

Him: Lol! Whatever. Don't stop. I'm not going anywhere.

Me: I know, but you are high on my friends list. Never forget that.

Him: One day I might get lucky.

Me: I just be overwhelmed sometimes and I don't like transferring that energy.

Him: I understand, Queen. I feel lucky when I get to see when I can.

Me: I'm about to soak. We'll catch up soon.

Him: Okay, enjoy.

Weeks go by and we hang out.

Him: Those fishnets. I'm a slave for those when they come out.

Me: I told you that I live in a whole other world. I purchase things most have never seen before.

Him: I love them…as I love you.

Me: Thank you. I love you too.

Him: You're welcome. Enjoy your night. I'm done being "thirsty."

Me: Thanks, you too. I'm about to go to bed.

Him: Okay goodnight.

Days later.

Him: I feel like a crackhead thinking about you the way that I do. I've been yearning for you like crazy.

Me: I've found that many women move differently than me. I feel bad for them. I've heard so many guys say how boring and lame many women are.

Him: The thing that gets to me is when these women say what they want from a man and never include what they have to offer. They want us to be the protector, provider, security, a maintenance man, and fuck good all night while they're on their backs. I mean…shit.

Me: Each person has to play their part. We all have to put in the work. It should never be one-sided. We have to take care of each other. People try to figure out how all my relationships have been so long. You have to offer more than ass. Personality, mental stimulation, and common sense play major factors.

Him: You said it best. On another note, I want to cuddle with you.

Me: Whatever. I don't believe that.

Him: I do. You already know that.

Me: Why?

Him: Just to get some good energy.

Me: What else are you trying to get?

Him: That's it.

Me: Uh huh. Sure. You want to be my sex slave, don't you?

Him: No, I want to soak up some of your energy. You're bad.

Me: Oh…we'll see. Tell me what you really want.

Him: Uh…fuck it. Next time that I see you, I'm sucking on those titties. I'm eating your pussy. I'm also sucking on those toes.

Me: Ooh I like that.

Him: I'm busting a nut on your face…now my dick is hard.

Me: You bad lil boy you.

Him: I'm going to fuck your face.

Me: Tasty lil boy you. Naughty lil boy you.

Him: I'll be all that.

Me: Freaky lil boy you.

Him: I'll do everything that you ask of me.

Me: I'm running.

Him: Nope. Not this time.

Me: Shut up before I make you unzip them pants and do what I want you to do!

Him: What if I tell you to make me do as I'm told? I'm coming to your car with no draws on.

Me: Car full of snow…body temperature causing it all to melt.

Him: Yes. Yes.

Me: Let me get ready for work and quit playing with you.

Him: Work on this dick.

Me: Bounce on it too?

Him: Yes, with my thumb in your butt.

Me: Now you're talking. Hahaha!! Let me get to work.

Him: Or a vibrator. Lol! Okay. You get to work. When I do see you the next time though, I'm making that pussy gush. I'm sure that I just gave you that second heartbeat.

Me: You don't know what I got. You should come see and listen for a second heartbeat.

Him: Let me taste you.

Me: Come lift up my skirt.

Him: Oh…you got a skirt on?

Me: Almost every day.

Him: No panties?

Me: I don't recall putting on any this morning. This conversation did not go as planned. I need to quit messing with your head like that. Have a relaxing day, sir.

Him: I wish that you could hop on my plate right now. I'm starving. You have belonged to me…since first sight.

Me: I'm too spoiled. I have to be taken care of, not just on a sexual and mental level, but on a financial level. I've got too much to lose.

Him: I understand. You think that I don't know this already? I got you on all of that.

He wants to reconnect.

Him: I'm going to give you a long hug.

Me: You better. It's going to be for at least 5 minutes.

Him: Hell yeah…cuddling standing up.

Me: Yes…you know that I love that shit.

Him: Me too.

Me: If I didn't have to work, you'd be meeting me right now.

Him: That would be so much love…bury my head in your chest and just listen to your heartbeat.

Me: Boy…you better quit. I'd sing you a lullaby with my heart and stroke your head with my hands.

Him: Oh shit!! Game over.

Me: I'd have your whole being jumping for joy.

Him: You already know that I know. I love your spirit.

Me: Thank you. I love all of you.

Him: …and all of me loves you.

Me: You better be good.

Him: I am good. I LOVE YOU!! I had to say it loud in the case you just forgot.

Me: I love you berry berry much. I just want to be respectful of you.

Him: You are respectful to me.

Me: I've been trying to be.

Him: You want to tie me up and be disrespectful to me deep down. Don't you?

Me: How did you know??

Him: I want you to stand over me and release those juices...all over me. Sorry. I just want that magical energy.

Me: I feel your requests all the time. Your soul energy taps into mine. I always knew that it was going to be like that though. No matter the time or the distance.

Him: Seriously? How is that?

Me: Do you feel your spirit being at peace when we're communicating with one another? Power source.

Him: Yes. Always. Thank you for transferring that good energy onto me. It fills me up...every time.

Me: I have to make you feel "mmm mmm good." I'm like your soup and vegetables.

Him: Well...I'm hungry now, so what are we going to do about that? I need to eat.

Me: Omg!! See.

Him: I do want to be super nasty.

Me: I don't know if I want to relax and stay away, or do cartwheels on you, or walk away completely. Man...decisions.

Him: We don't have to be. The thought of it is enough. I would let you do anything to me though.

Me: For now, I'll just stare at you over my teacup when we meet up.

Him: Lol! Okay.

Me: I'll bring my gadgets in the case that I change my mind.

Him: We are going to be good. I would let you give me a golden shower.

Me: Really?! Don't play with me like that.

Him: Lol! Have a good day ma'am.

Me: Let me get myself together before I do something to you. Have a peaceful day, sir.

Him: Yeah…some freaky shit. I would let you have your way.

Me: I've been keeping my cool for a long time. You know this…

Him: Cool is good. What's something that you want to try?

Me: I want one of those boards where you tie up the hands and the wrists while the guy's legs are spread apart. I want a real dungeon.

Him: Is that right? What else would you do? You have to get creative.

Me: I still want to paint…with honey.

Him: That's going to be a mess.

Me: I will even drop some marshmallows and watch them stick too. I'll be sure to clean it up with my being. Messy is good.

Him: Then you're going to taste it??

Me: I can't tell all my secrets. You know this already.

Him: How would you shower on me?

Me: I want to use crushed pineapples too…with the 100% fruit juices.

Him: Ohhh shit!!!

Me: You'd be lying on your back, with your head tilted back, me hovering over you, with me starting at the ends of your feet, and me working my way to the top of your face.

Him: I love you so much, woman!! I swear that I do!!

Octo-Man

I want you to use all of your limbs

If it were up to me, I'd give you more of them

I want you using your hands, arms, legs, head, neck, and
feet simultaneously

I want you rubbing my feet while your tongue is playing
with my pussy

Switching positions, I want your hands lifting my ass while
your legs are standing sturdily and you watching me from
behind

Flip me over and hold me down by my thighs

Kiss and nibble on my "FUPA," telling her how much you
adore her

Rub the tips of my fingers with your fingertips

Lick and suck on the pads of my toes while you're playing
with my other holes

Pull on my hair by the roots while jerking me toward you

Bend my body into acrobatic positions

Sit me on your balancing beam

Bounce me while my breasts shake and shiver

Quench your thirst from the drops of me

Comforter

Him: What's yo plan for the day?

Me: Other than going to the gym later, nothing, surprisingly. What about you?

Him: I don't know either.

Me: Uh oh, sounds like somebody is looking for trouble.

Him: Only if it's with you.

Me: I'd love to catch up and chat…it's been a while.

Him: I know.

Me: I see that someone is growing into their manhood. Keep it up.

Him: Thank you. I'm trying.

Me: Yes, you're welcome.

Him: I like your style. Since we were kids, you've always kept yourself presentable and like a lady. I love that about you…you're classy.

Me: Thank you, friend. I was going to shut it down at the party too, but I didn't want to do 'em like that lol.

Him: Lmao…you looked nice. I was surprised when I saw you at the party. I almost never get to run into you anymore.

Me: I appreciate that.

Him: No doubt. You know that I had to show you some love.

Me: Yep, it's still love this way too.

Him: Glad to know that. It was nice seeing you.

Me: It was nice seeing you too, mi amigo.

Him: That's what's up. I still remember the nickname that I gave you.

Me: I'll never forget it either. I guess that it'll forever be mine.

Him: I don't want to start any trouble with calling you that.

Me: Naw, I don't have any cuffs on me, so you can't get me into trouble.

Him: Hahaha! Stop it.

Me: I'll behave for now.

Him: Don't start nothing that you can't finish.

Me: What I really think is that you want to get bitten…you're just scared to ask.

Him: Bitten? What do you mean?

Me: Oh…you know. Don't you? Do you want to get bit? I am a lioness.

Him: What does bit mean?

Me: Loved on.

Him: So you wanna bite me?

Me: I'm not answering that.

Him: You said that I'm scared to ask, so I asked.

Me: Yeah…you got me there. My answer is perhaps.

Him: I don't know what perhaps mean.

Me: Hahaha! Never mind.

Him: In other words, be real with me. No beating behind the bush.

Me: You make me bashful, so I can't answer that.

Him: Why do I make you bashful? What did I do?

Me: I don't know why. You just do.

Him: You never in your life had a hard time telling me nothing.

Me: At times I did. You are a changed man now though, so I don't want to interfere. You're growing and I don't want to interrupt that.

Some days pass.

Him: Happy Holidays!

Me: Thanks and Happy Holidays to you too!

Him: Thanks. What are you getting into?

Me: Yes, you're welcome. I have to work today and possibly tomorrow.

Him: I'm fresh off of work.

Me: You suck. I'm jealous.

Him: Lol. Whatever.

Me: Enjoy your time off.

Him: I will.

He tells me a funny joke.

Me: I can't stand you! That's how you be talking about people??

Him: Ha!! No, that's all you.

Me: Yep…sometimes. I can't help that I'm goofy.

Him: That's the best way to be. How you been though? How has life been treating you?

Me: You got that right. We're grown kids in the best way. I've been good, mostly working and educating myself daily. I'm always making time for the family…you know that's always. I'll be having a party soon. You know that I like to host parties. I'll be sure to send you an invite. You can bring some of your people too if you'd like. How is life for you and your people? Thanks for asking, by the way.

Him: Congratulations on all of your accomplishments. You've always been about your business and educating yourself. I've been good, I just want to be mentally strong and educated as well. I want to stay young forever but get wiser at the same time. I have business plans for myself. I want to have a drive like you to persevere.

Me: Thanks so much! It feels good that others recognize my hard work. I wish you all the best with all your endeavors. You are a brilliant person. You will always do well in whatever you choose.

Him: Thank you. I appreciate it. Yeah, I ain't trying to be slaving until I'm 79, so I'm trying to make wise decisions while I'm young. Nope...not trying to do that.

Me: I can just see it now. Many many years from now, your ass is going to be on the retired cruise ship sleeping like a mother fucker with your straw hat on and your margarita sitting next to you. Hahaha!!

Him: Yep...hopefully next year lol.

Me: Good. You're on it early.

Him: On another note...I'm always the one to check on you. What's up with that?

Me: I told you that I don't want to hinder your growth. I want to be respectful. I just know to be careful with you and limit my communication. I don't want anything serious and I know that you're a relationship guy. It's only my honesty. You know that I'm a free spirit.

Him: I feel you. What are you about to get into today?

Me: I have some reading to do. I may watch a movie also, which is something that I rarely do or have time for.

Him: What's been new in your world?

Me: Well, you know me. I love to create and inspire. I'm always getting into something. How about yourself?

Him: I've been focusing on some new business ideas. Maybe you can help me some. We should meet up sometime to discuss them when we both have some more free time. I just want to be financially free. I've always valued our friendship. We've been cool for a long time…since we were teens.

Me: Yes, I've always valued yours too. That's why I made an effort to come visit you at least once a month back in the day. We will always be good friends no matter what.

Him: Yes you did come to visit me, but then the visits stopped.

Me: The visits stopped because I got tired of my visits being interrupted by your crazy-ass chicks! The calls, pop-ups, driving past your house, etc. was too much for me.

Him: Huh?? Yeah right. I don't remember that. I never had any stalkers.

Me: Oh yes there were. I could throw out a few names of some of them. That's not something someone would typically forget.

Him: I don't know why some of those girls were acting so crazy. Some of them I never was even intimate with.

Me: Oh okay. It was just weird and you always seemed paranoid like they were on some "Spiderman" type shit and would climb into your bedroom window.

Him: My shit wasn't even that good to have stalkers.

Me: I still remember how you look when I was on top and when you would cum. But I digress. I'm done. Those days are behind me now.

Him: We had some fun times.

Me: Yeah we did. Most importantly, though, I enjoyed the laughs and the cuddles more than anything.

Him: You were the first and only girl that I did uniquely freaky shit to. You taught me a few tricks.

Me: Wait a min. The only?

Him: Yup. You are creative…I'm talking about next level. It was never a dull moment. I can't say that about other women.

Me: So you're telling me that I got a gold star engraved in these streets…like the walk of fame?

Him: You actually made me cum in other ways outside of intercourse or oral. Never thought I'd cum off of some titties, but I think that your facial expressions is what made me cum. Yes…you do have a gold star.

Me: I am the female "Bruce Leroy." My name is Leah Bruche.

Him: Haaaa!! Shut up!! I still know your number by heart.

Me: You always will remember it. There's no way to get me out of your head.

Him: Lol! Shut up! You know that you're always thinking about me.

Me: Eh…I used to. A lot. You just wasn't willing to do everything that I liked. I wanted you to explore a little bit more. I'm a Dom.

Him: I know. Back then, I wasn't ready for all that. My pride was everything.

Me: Yeah, you were young. Well…you're still young, just not as young. You know what I'm trying to say. I realized that I was a little more advanced and risky then. I think that I got most of it out of my system now. I was a sex addict then.

Him: I'm an addict now.

Me: Being a sex addict is one hell of a drug.

Him: Tell me about it. I got a problem.

Me: The only way to really overcome it is to go through withdrawal and keep yourself busy doing other things. At one point I was having sex 2–3 times a day. Nobody could keep up with me.

Him: The women that I was with couldn't keep up with me either. I just dealt with it. Just know that you and I will always be friends for life.

Me: Yes, you'll always be one of my friends. I don't say that about too many people.

Him: I better be or we will fight.

Me: Oh hush. I can get upset with you anytime that I want, but it will never last.

Him: Right. You always had a weak spot for me. I don't know what it is about me.

Me: I sure did and still do. I loved how you love on your family as much as you do. I also like how you try to see the good in everyone. I never saw you throw hate on anyone. I also liked how you treated me during the times I'd be at your place visiting you. It was rough for me during my years, but I felt at peace with you.

Him: Awww man…I'm seriously about to cry. You always do something to my soul.

Me: I'm sorry. It's the truth though.

Him: Don't be sorry. You have always been positive and rocked with me. We will be homies for life, so if you need me, I got you.

Me: Thank you, sugar. Likewise. I said that I'd always rock with you and I meant that.

Him: I know. I don't think that we ever fell out or beefed with each other.

Me: No, we haven't, which is rare, especially considering the age group that we're in. People our age always are bickering about something. I'm just glad that we're still learning and growing mentally. Friends for life.

Him: That's for sure. It will always be that way. I hope that you have an amazing rest of the day…even if it doesn't include me in it later on.

Me: Thanks much. You enjoy your day as well.

Him: But I will say that I know that you miss "it."

Me: To be honest, I don't miss "it." I like the other "pleasures" of life. Besides…you could never keep up with me. I like that adventurous shit. You know…the wild side of things.

Ice Cube

Look at what you made me do!

I've melted all over you…all in your mustache…all in your beard.

I can see a few drops on your bottom lip appearing as honeydew. I've gotten myself all over you.

I can see the imprints of your fingerprints on the sides of my thighs from you holding them way high…so high.

I started out in your mouth as a glistening diamond ice cube…now look at you.

My shape has been reformed.

I can feel the pulse of me on your tongue.

I push on the inside and you catch every beat in your mouth.

How sweet the taste is to you.

My pheromones are like soft scented incense in the room.

I ask for you to dip your stick in the aroma and then light it up.

Waver that sweet scent into the air.

Breathe it all in.

Be one with all of me.

The Game

Him: Do you want to meet at our spot?

Me: Yes, I can meet you there. Give me 20 mins, then I'll be ready to
    head your way.

    I grab my keys, my purse, and then make my way to my vehicle. The drive seems long...real long. The distance only seems like it is so far due to the butterflies that flutter, dance, and sing "Ring Around the Rosie" at the pit of my stomach. I pull up, look around, breathe, and then turn my body toward the driver door. I step out. I feel the warm sun on my skin. The weather is perfect. It is about seventy-five degrees out in the late afternoon. I walk through the grass, looking down at the pace of my feet. I try not to walk too fast, yet try not to take forever to get to him. I occasionally alternate between looking down at my feet and looking up at him from a distance. He looks so small since I am so far away. Before I know it, he is big and in plain sight.

    He greets me with "Hey. How are you, love?"

    My response is "I'm well. Thanks for asking. How have you been these days?"

    Literally minutes after we've been sitting and looking across the field of grass, three deer come trailing by us. I am so fascinated. I begin to smile. He then reflects a smile off of mine. Our eyes end up locking and all I can see is him wanting to eat me...eat me whole. I don't speak one word of my thoughts. I don't need to. He reads everything that I am thinking.

I sit next to him and tuck my body into his. He smells so damn good. I lay my head against his chest. I nuzzle in closer, then told him, "It feels like somebody was missing me."

He says, "Well, from the looks and feels of it, somebody missed me too."

I then ask him, "So…did you miss me?"

His response is "Of course. I always do." He then turns on the music from his device. Shortly after he turns on the music, he asks me to face him. He looks me up and down. He then begins to move one side of my dress over to the side. He starts to rub on my outer thigh, which leads to him rubbing on the inside of my thigh. He makes sure that he grips all the firm skin and thick-ass meat that his hand can hold. I see the bottom of his lip hide behind his teeth as he does this.

As I look further across the field, I can see some people playing a game. They pay us no attention. In fact, I doubt that they would even notice that we are there because we are so far away from them. I draw my attention away from the others and back onto him. He asks me to lay my back and head against his chest. He grabs both sides of my hips and slides my lower body down. As he does that, he reaches his right arm and hand to my legs. He slowly slides up my dress so that he can feel my "Honey Love." With a few of his fingers, he starts rubbing on her.

My back and head are still lying against his chest. My lower body is in between his legs, which he begins to play with his hand. The more he plays with her, the more my love potion begins to pour. He dips his fingers in her and then brings his hand to his face. He sniffs his fingers long and hard. A few times, actually, and says, "Oooh, baby, you smell so fucking good." He then puts one of his fingers to his mouth and says, "…and you taste good too." He asks me if he can taste my "Honey Love" all the way.

I tell him, "Absolutely." I tell him that we'll have to leave in order for him to finish eating her. He says that we are good where we are. I laugh it off, thinking that he is joking. In fact, he couldn't be more serious.

At this time about an hour has passed and the temperature has dropped some degrees. It is beginning to get a breeze. Luckily I brought a button-up sweater with me. I am prepared for the weather. I tell him that the breeze is getting to me.

He says, "You might as well let the breeze run across Ms. Kitty too." He lifts my dress once more so that I can feel the crisp air caress her as he is caressing me. I let him. It all feels so fucking good. He tells me to turn and face him so that he can finish tasting her.

I say to him, "Are you crazy?! What if someone sees us?"

He says that no one is paying any attention to us. He says, "Let's have some fun. You deserve it. You've been working hard and have been stressed all week. You need to treat yourself. Just relax and open your legs." I sit in my thoughts for a moment and reflect on his words and on my long, stressful week. Eventually I make up my mind. The only thing that I want at that moment is to look down and see the top of his head in my lap. He asks me for my sweater. I ask him if he is cold and he tells me, "No, I'm going to cover your lap with it." I am taken aback with smiles and rays of sunshine building up inside of me. He says, "Lie back." I am mesmerized as I listen to a song called "So Anxious" play in the background. I can see the beautiful clouds drifting in front of me. The formation of the clouds even smiles at me…I swear.

He is saying something while he is down there, but I can't hear him. All of a sudden I feel a tap on my thigh and I hear him say, "Get up, get up. Just stay cool though."

I slowly get up and he leans me close to him and then says, "Don't look, but there's a guy standing across from us." He thinks it's funny and silently begins to laugh. At this moment, I go into mental panic mode, wondering if the man noticed what he was doing. He tells me to relax and says, "I told you to watch cover from your angle. Didn't you hear me when I was talking to you while I was between those thick-ass juicy thighs?" I start to laugh and tell him that I couldn't make out what he was saying. At this moment, my natural high has come down and I'm ready to head back home.

Tangled

You tilt my head back.

My neck is lightly gripped from behind with one hand.

The other hand has loose twists wrapped around each of your fingers.

You yank just enough to get my full attention.

I'm commanded to listen to the sound of your voice.

You instruct me to dip my back downward into the bed.

I listen and obey.

A light smack on my ass is followed by a kiss on my shoulder.

I moan.

That moan is followed by several other moans from me and you.

My hair is still in your hand.

I reach my arms back to pull your face closer to mine.

My mind is tangled and hanging on to you.

My body is tangled and intertwined with you.

We are both tangled into each other.

Alfredo

It was the season of fall. I was asked if I wanted to spend the day with him. I accepted his invitation. We were going on our first date together. He insisted on picking me up from my place. We had grown to know each other over the phone, so I didn't feel like he was a stranger. We had seen each other physically prior, but it wasn't anything serious or on a romantic level. We started out as friends. He was mad cool. I'd even call him a sweetheart. He was always checking on me. I liked that most about him. He was consistent. You don't meet too many men that would wait months on end to go on a date.

So I started to get ready for our date. I made sure that I was looking cute, but not overdoing it. Instead of wearing lipstick, I went for the lip gloss. Instead of wearing my hair down, I put it up in a ponytail. I wanted him to learn me first. I didn't want to move too fast. I wanted him to know the inner core of me. I was planning to have a long conversation with this man. This one was something special. I could feel him differently than I felt the other guys. I wanted to take my time with him.

He called me to let me know that he was getting ready to head out to pick me up. I replied, "Thank you. I'm ready." He pulled up and had the cutest smile and whitest teeth that I had seen on a man. His smile was perfection. His eyes looked like tea mixed with honey. They were a soft light brown. I still remember the smell of his vehicle. The scent was fresh. His music was blasting…I'm guessing that he was trying to impress me. I love to hear a good tune. Music is my thing.

I got into the car bashfully. I was hoping to have a good evening. He asked me if I needed to stop anywhere before we headed to his place. I thought that was a nice gesture. I realized that he was always offering to take me where I needed to go. Not many are willing to drive you around like that. I told him that I was good at the moment. We then pulled up to his place. Once I walked in, I immediately sat down on the couch. He offered me something to drink, giving various options. As I sat there, he told me that he was about to prepare dinner. He said, "I hope that you like chicken alfredo." In fact, I love it.

He started pulling out all of these spices and ingredients. I couldn't believe that this young guy was about to prepare me a meal from scratch...and on the first date at that. I didn't have to lift a finger. I just sat there and looked pretty. He was precise with his culinary skills. The veggies that he picked out were bright and fresh. He sautéed them in light extra-virgin olive oil. The chicken was also sautéed. The seasonings had his place filled with aromas. I was ready to eat from just the smell of it alone. He even had soapy water in the sink for the dishes that he was using. I was impressed. It showed me that he knew what he was doing. Once the food was prepared, he served my dish to me. I didn't have to get up for anything. I took a forkful and it was "love at first bite." The taste was so savory. It had a lot of sauce, which I liked. He even prepared garlic bread and salad to go with the chicken alfredo. I'm not much of a bread person, but the thought was sweet. He seemed so caring. After dinner, we continued to talk some more. The idea of intimacy was never brought up. He was a total gentleman. We were there together for at least four hours in conversation.

As the night went on, I started to get sleepy. I asked if he was ready to take me back home. He said that he didn't want the night to end, but that he understood I needed my rest. He reached for his jacket and keys. I gathered my purse and headed toward the door. Before I

158

met the door, I turned around, looked him up and down, and said, "You aren't going to ask me for a kiss before I leave?"

The look on his face was priceless. He was in shock. He was shy. He gave me a slight grin and said, "Well…I wasn't going to, but since you were the one to bring it up… Hell yeah I want a kiss." We connected in a passionate kiss in his doorway. I had my back against the door. The kiss went on for several minutes. Neither one of us wanted to let go of each other.

Eventually we did. I thanked him for a pleasant evening and complimented him on his cooking skills. I reached for the doorknob and he said, "When I'm around, you will never touch a door." I was made speechless by how well-mannered he was. I was hoping that it wasn't a facade and that he was genuinely a gentleman.

* * *

I bring him peace while others bring him chaos.

NutCrackHER

Watching my thick thighs save their nine lives.

They tighten and grip, waiting to crack that nut.

Fill me up like a glass of water.

I want to make you forget how you even got here.

Your mind is in another realm of life.

Did you die or did you cum alive?

You have no idea how you got here.

I'll always make sure that you remember…every
time.

I reach and grab you from all angles that can be
touched and physically untouched.

I tap into every core of you until you tap out.

I love you too much to let you go out like that.

I'll bring you back.

I breathe air into you as if you never left.

Egg

I lean up against your soul.

I look up and see you clearly.

I'm admiring you.

Not just some…but your whole entire being.

I knock on your wall.

A sudden crack begins to form.

I wonder what's held behind it…behind you?

Are you hiding from me? Are you hiding from
yourself?

I'm on a mission to discover you…again…all of you.

Studio Luvin

All day he had been trying to get my attention. He asked, "Hey, where are you? Are you still coming thru?" I told him that I was near, but I had to make a few runs first. In my mind I was smiling from ear to ear. I'd always wanted to know what it was like getting head while leaning up against a switchboard. I was really about to experience my passion and love for music. All of the high notes were going to be let out. No one was going to hear the sounds of my music but him and me.

Before I pulled up, I called him to let him know that I'd be arriving in a few short minutes. I was nervous and excited at the same time once I did get there. It was sunny today. I could've gone to one of my favorite outdoor hiding spots, but today I chose to be with him. I wanted to see what adventurous displays of affection he had in store for me instead. This should be fun.

Once I got out of the car and walked up the stairs, I was greeted by him. He was punctual. I liked that about him. He knew not to waste my time. I don't take any minute for granted. He said to me, "Come in. Relax. Make yourself as comfortable as you want to be." I asked him where the restroom was located and he showed me. It was clean and it smelled good. The studio was also clean. All of the instruments looked so beautiful. I even walked into one of the studio booths. I can't sing, but if I could, I would be utilizing this space right now.

Eventually I walked over to where he was standing. He had no words once I reached him. He was literally staring me up and down. I could feel exactly what he wanted to do to me and with me. I wanted him to. I wanted him to do what he wanted to do with his mouth. He knew it was my favorite. He didn't forget what I told him to do. He grabbed me by my ass and pulled me closer to him. I had on tights under my dress. He lifted my dress up and slid my tights down simultaneously. I watched him. I watched how his face lit up knowing that he would get to have some of the sweetest nectar that ever dripped on earth. He pivoted me so that my body leaned up against a board. His eyes connected with mine. Our stare was intense. He wasted no time going down. He said almost nothing. He knew how to get to work. The orgasmic rush that I felt could not be expressed in words. I'll just say that it was a feeling I'd never felt and a sound I'd never heard come out of myself. The intensity was everything. It was hard to keep my eyes open after our session. I was overtaken with fatigue from orgasming so hard. I had to force myself to get to the restroom to freshen up. My legs felt like I was a baby deer walking for the first time. My legs felt so heavy. I told him that I needed to leave to get some other things done on my agenda. He was understanding. He didn't pressure me to let him penetrate. Some guys wouldn't let me slide like that. He was a gentleman. I liked that about him too.

Before I left, I gave him a kiss on his cheek. He smiled and thanked me. I said, "No. Thank you, sir. You're the one that did all the work. The only thing that I had to do was sit back and enjoy you pleasing me." He told me that most of his pleasure was seeing me be pleased and that was all that mattered.

I did one last walk-through once I was able to stand and keep my legs from shaking. I admired the guitars the most. The drum set, trumpet, and saxophone appeared as if they'd been recently dusted. They looked clean and I could tell that they had been put to good use.

Sometimes you have to smell and kiss the rose at the same time.

Soup

Take your spoon.

Get all the nourishment and vegetables that you need.

Make sure that you blow off the heat before you
scoop me into your mouth.

There may be drizzles on your chin and lip.

Take your napkin, lightly dab, and clean yourself up.

Did you get enough?

Are you full?

Are you satisfied?

Do you need bread and butter to go with it?

Or am I enough?

Mr. Seduction

He sent me a message that said, *Stay close to people who feel like sunlight*, and told me that he was trying to do just that. I was told that he missed me. I echoed his words, saying, *I miss you*. We went on about vivid memories.

Him: You are so damn beautiful. You were right. I will always miss you. I want to call you so bad, but I remember our last conversation.

I thanked him and said: We are still good people. I miss my friend as well. We can still occasionally check on each other.

Me: Oh yeah, the best part about it is that we never had any bad times, so my memories of us together will always be good. So…when I really miss you, I think about those times.

Him: Yes, you're right. I love that the most…the fact that we've never had a fallout. I wish you nothing but the best. I wish you all the happiness in the world, but when you see me, you better not act like you don't know me. What it all boils down to is, you will always have a friend in me.

I told him that I would never do that. I respected him too much to do that.

Him: I'm about to let you go now until I need my life coach again or just some good advice.

Me: When I go into therapy, I'll let you know, so that you can become one of my clients. Seriously though.

Me: Have a peaceful weekend.

Him: Always remember you will always be my Sunshine.

Me: Thanks for always being a sweetheart to me.

Him: You know that you're my wife…in a different time and space, right?

Me: I am?

Him: Yes. The Multiverse or maybe a past life.

Me: Perhaps. I'll never know. The thought is nice though.

Him: Yes it is.

Him: So…will it be a rare thing that I'll be able to see you? You were my only something back then. I told you that I have to trust who I spend my time with. That's rare these days out here. So now, my only naughty memories are with you and I'm content with that.

Me: I feel you all the way. People are quick to be deceitful and will tarnish you. Even when it comes to friends, I only see a few people. Most times I'm with family. But oh…what memories we have.

Him: My memory is with no one else. I'm thinking once upon a time when I was a little frustrated with you.

Me: I know. I saw it in your soul through your eyes. I know how much you love the one that you're with, which is why I'm always walking away from you when you approach me. You weren't able to walk away from me. I saw your infatuation with me through your eyes. I don't want to be selfish or stingy. I have to leave some for the rest of the world. But…I know that you loved her more.

Him: …and you weren't in the same boat?!

Me: Correct. We were both in love with other people.

Him: I still have no regrets.

Me: Me either. Our moments were more than amazing. You were my comfort.

Him: You were my grown-up crush. Actually, you still are.

Me: Yes…always will be.

Him: All my memories of us in my mind seem like one long passionate night that started out at a park and ended up at my house.

Me: You stand corrected.

Him: I just want my friend back.

I told him that I never stopped being his friend. Our downtime always conflicted due to our schedules.

He apologized and said: You're right. You're a good friend as a matter of fact. The reason being is because you always make it possible to be there for me when I need you the most.

Me: I promise to be there for you during your darkest moments… always.

We ended up setting up a date to meet for lunch on a friendly level. Once we connected, he said: *I just want you to make sure that you don't forget about me.*

Me: I never will. You loved on me in unique ways, so it's hard to forget you even if I wanted to.

Him: I believe that you were made for me. I just didn't live the life I was meant to live to be prepared for you. I hope that the guy that you're dating realizes how lucky he truly is.

I don't think that he initially realized what he had at one point in time, but I feel that he does now.

Me: You always said that I was made for you. Sometimes I do think about that. I'm spoiled and sometimes I want it all. For now, I want you to focus on her. Thanks for making my soul happy during the moments that we did have.

How?

How do you feel someone that can't be touched?

How do you smell a fragrance that has long lingered in the wind?

How do you taste the sweetness of their kiss that's been given long ago?

How do you visualize togetherness that was never present?

How do you see the eyes staring at you that are miles away in the distance?

How can you touch the soft beautiful skin that has slipped away from your hands?

How can you caress the warmth of someone whose hugs aren't shown?

How do you walk away from love that will be waiting for you on the other end?

How do you learn patience when time is always limited?

How do you give the most precious gift to someone who has everything that they need?

How do you be kind to a heart that will never be yours?

How do you love knowing that love has to eventually walk away?

Head Fantasies

He asked me: What are you doing? Ma'am…are you trying to starve
    me?

My reply: I have been.

Him: Why is that? You need to bring me some cake.

Me: Would you stop being nasty for once?

Him: Oh…so you're not nasty no more?

I ignore him for a few weeks.

I asked him: You mad at me?

Him: Why should I be?

Me: Well…since I haven't been letting you be bad with me.

Him: No, I'm not mad at you, Queen. So you're thinking of me? I'm
    assuming that you were referring to my mouth being on your
    pussy?

Me: Thinking about you…not your mouth.

Him: You better not be roaring for nobody but me…

Me: How are you going to act? You make women roar all the time.
    Don't make demands of me.

Him: Not me…your roar is mine.

Me: Sure. Sure.

Him: You don't give a fuck about being my love…and that's OK. But
    my feelings are not based on yours.

Me: You have enough loves. You don't need to be worried about me. On another topic, how is your day going?

Him: I dropped them. I'm tired of that shit. I want you...you know that.

Me: Why are you tired of them?

Him: They get no attention if you're present. I don't like them. They're weak to me. They aren't you. They don't have what I need, but you have everything that I need...and want. I run into good women...I just don't feel them on that other level. It's not like it is with you. You are undeniable magnetic attraction.

Me: Really? So that's how you see me?

Him: When will you be free for me?

Me: Today. Act accordingly and follow my ground rules.

Him: You know that I'll obey each and every one of your commands. If I could, I'd stay in bed with you forever. You are my Lioness. If you allow me 10 spankings that would be nice too.

Me: Spankings? I'm not sure if that will be allowed today. We will see.

Him: ...and when I messaged you last night, I was so fucking horny thinking about you. In my mind, you were getting fucking and sucking on a fat dick. I was like...super turned on. I nutted at least three times and moaned your name twice. That was just an FYI.

Me: You are a terrible mess.

Him: I'm your mess, baby. Come nut in my mouth please. If you're gonna show off, then show off. Me: You got it...don't be so "conservative."

Me: I'm being conservative?

Him: Yup. Very cute…very safe. But…you want to do more. I can see it in your eyes.

Me: So you can read me now?

Him: I can read chapters in you that you didn't know were in your book.

Me: Like? Do tell.

Him: If I tell you, then you're gonna try to take them out of your book. I'll keep it to myself for now.

Me: Oh hush!

Him: I was right obviously.

Me: Tell me!

Him: Tell you what?

Me: Your version of my story. As you say…my chapters.

Him: I'll whisper it in your ear while I spank your big pretty ass. Keep acting like you don't want it.

Me: I'm not about to go there with you today.

Him: We should go every day. You need to cum feed me.

I send him a quote that I saw: Be the reason someone is motivated or smiles or masturbates today. Whatever works.

Him: You too.

A few months go by.

Him: I miss you, damn! Can you be sweet? Yes, I do miss you, babe, and I ain't have no hoes or whatever you're going to claim that I fucked. Do you plan on pimping me forever?"

Me: Well…that's kind of what I do.

Him: Just come on and do what you're supposed to do. I promise that I'll be a good boy.

Me: Nope.

Him: Damn…it's simple. The buffoonery shall continue.

Me: Nope. I'm just over here with my eyes on my bank accounts.

Him: Greedy ass.

Me: All the time. You need to get comfortable in the seat of neglect. Your ass is crazy.

Him: Wow! How am I crazy? 'Cause I miss the rain? Women… just… y'all are some dogs, man! Y'all don't care about us men… it's sad!

Me: What do you mean you miss me? You didn't do anything to keep me.

Him: Really?? So you're lying today? So you want it bought and not kept? That's ludicrous. You're still my baby though.

Me: You ain't never spoiled me like no damn baby. Stop it.

Him: I was licking your pussy and letting you cum in my beard…you wanted more than that? You have to relax. Cut it out. You're supposed to love me and this is what you do.

Me: Love on me and spoil me, then things might change.

Him: I'll spoil you with non-monetary things that lovers use to spoil one another with. Damn…you're acting like I haven't tried for us to move in together. I've got bill money ready. I like romance, sweetness, surprises, time, energy, etc. I like all of that.

Me: You can still put money on bills without staying. I can get love from an animal. Love can be found almost anywhere. Being spoiled only comes in limited forms.

Him: An animal ain't about to eat them guts and hold your spoiled ass when you're on your soapbox talking about how much we live in a fucked-up society. You also need your rubdowns.

Me: Damn…you got me.

Him: Exactly. Now can I have you? Damn.

Me: You always know how to get to me. I can't stand your ass.

Him: Now cum bust open that pot of gold.

Me: As good as that sounds…nope.

Him: I like it better when you take forever. Anyways, I'll let it marinate. I'm talking about "falling off the bone and melting in my mouth."

Me: As En Vogue said, "Never gonna get it. Never gonna get it."

Him: I love it! I hate to sound easy, but tease me.

Me: Nope.

Him: I'll keep your slot open.

Me: You can sew it up. The slot is not needed.

Him: I'll keep it open anyway. You can be my Queen B.

Me: I'm not going to keep going back and forth about that. You're a single man with any single women to choose from. You have yourself a beautiful day.

Him: Geesh! Enjoy the elements, my Sister. The moon is aligned with the Osiris solar system…and "Ol Dirty Bastard" is in the rotation.

Me: Shut up! Lol!

Him: Lol! I knew that you were gonna feel the essence from my spirit eroding the equation, my Sister!

Me: I know that you miss me, baby…have a good day. That's not cool to mock the "culture" the way that you just did…and you know that too lol!

Him: The culture is all over my Sister…we precede the ancient wisdoms.

Me: You got me rocking in the chair from laughter! Would you just quit it with this shit?!

Someone asked me what I be doing to these men. My response was, "Everything they want and don't want to be done."

Because You Loved Me

Because you loved me despite my circumstances.

You loved me unconditionally when I was in an unstable mental and physical state of not being able to love myself.

You literally brought life back into me.

You cared for me as if I were a newborn child.

You even brought me soup to help me feel better.

You made sure to find ways to help me laugh and smile.

You even made me smile with my eyes.

You kissed my pain and tears away.

I'll forever be grateful for that.

You loved me like no man has done in my entire life.

We went fishing, went on walks, and drove around the state.

You even watched the rain fall with me, to help me fall out of my pain.

You rode all over the city during your downtime to meet and greet with me.

I appreciate your positive energy, love, and affection.

You make some of the best dishes a girl could ever want (so flavorful).

Food is the way to my heart.

You pray with me all the time.

I love that you love the Creator as much as I do.

You even held my hands when we prayed.

No man has ever done that with me either.

Ministry

Him: I see that you're giving them something special, huh?

Me: Just a little sprinkle of extra.

Him: Can I get some more extra please?

Me: I know what you want…Pastor.

Him: Lmbo. Listen to you.

Me: Am I lying?

Him: Lying about what?

Me: What you want.

Him: I had no expectations of anything. I like to think that I can give nice compliments to a beautiful woman without falling into the same lane as a whole lot of thirsty disrespectful brothers.

Me: OK, I'll fall back on my original thoughts. Thanks for your transparency.

Him: I'm not blind, but people are just waiting for me the "Passa"…lol…to misstep! I just wanna be able to give a compliment just like everyone else is allowed to, but I have dodged the gunfire, you know.

Me: I get it. I come from a religious background. I've always been a free spirit and enjoy the "taboos" of life. I get backlash for some of the things that I do, but give no fucks about how others think of it. You do deserve your kind of happiness like everyone else.

Him: True…so that's the connection that I have with you (religious background).

Me: Ironically, I'm not a Christian though. I've stepped away from religion for my own personal reasons. I consider myself spiritual and I do believe in God…just not the "church."

Him: The "church" is a building.

Me: Exactly.

Him: You'll find that I'm a different type of bringer of the Word of God.

Me: I see it already. I do enjoy the humor that you bring as well. You keep me laughing. How old are you by the way?

Him: I'll be 50 soon.

Me: I'm much younger, but my soul has been here before. I don't vibe with many my age.

Him: You look great. You're gorgeous.

Me: I do work out to keep my body toned. I move around as much as possible, which helps.

Him: So wait…quick question. Do you think that I was trying to get close and comfortable with you? I guess that I can't blame you for thinking it if you were. I'm sure that you get it all the time.

Me: Yeah pretty much. But you are always respectful to me, which is why I don't mind giving you conversation occasionally.

Him: Oh…lucky me.

Me: Yes, I guess that you can consider yourself a lucky man.

Him: Hey, you might find yourself the lucky one too you know.

Me: Really?! How so?

Him: I'm not sure yet, but I wasn't going to let your ego have all the shine. I'm gonna get some too.

Me: See...that humor and that charm that you have gets women's attention.

Him: Hahaha! Nah, not me.

Me: We are straight savages.

Him: Savages? I could take that word a lot of ways.

Me: You're the wildest of them all. Am I right? You thrive off of adventure, which is why you're interested in conversing with me. You know that I'm adventurous, which is why you've been led to me.

Him: Interesting...I do like adventures. I have to keep it in check for sure.

Me: Are we in a safe place?

Him: I tell people that they're as safe as they want to be. I do want you to know that I admire you. I admire everything that you do. You are beautifully sexy and fine.

Me: Your humor and charm is going to "take me to the King" or perhaps right to you. I know that your compliments are all in fun. They're graciously appreciated.

Him: You are welcome. They are in fun but nonetheless very very TRUE!

Me: Oh...I believe all of you.

Him: Good.

Me: I get it now. You want me to sprinkle some raindrops on you...don't you?

Him: Lmbo…raindrops?? Clever enough to make me think. I know what you mean, but I second-guess it at the same time. I will say that I've never been the sprinkle type. I'm more so "toe in the water" type. I just walk right in the rain. It's pretty refreshing. But…once again, I have no idea what you were referring to.

Me: Let me make sure that I'm clear. So you'd rather just jump and splash right into the puddles?

Him: Not so much splash…I'm just not scared to get wet.

Me: I have to put my head down for a second. See…I'm going to have to put myself in timeout for the thought that just popped up in my head.

Him: Really??

Me: Yes sir.

Him: Interesting. Well, if you ever want to share, let me know.

Me: Share my thoughts or my body?

Him: Your thoughts.

Me: Oh…my bad. Silly me. If I get a change of heart, I'll let you know.

Him: All right. Just know that I'm a great place to be.

Me: How great? Tell me in inches. I mean tell me on a scale from 1 to 10 (one being the least satisfied and 10 being the most satisfied).

Him: Satisfied for who?

Me: You know yourself better than I do. You tell me.

Him: I've never had complaints from anyone that I submitted my full work to. Never.

Me: So what kind of work do you enjoy most? What are your favorite positions? I mean…like what type of work have you done?

Him: I was a production manager for years so I'm well experienced in making sure that not only are production standards met, but quality is always above par. I am well versed in multiple positions on the line…in, above, below, and beyond.

Me: Nicely played. I enjoy stage plays. You make sure that everyone knows their roles and practice their scripts. You also make sure that they're standing, facing, and looking in all the right directions…putting in long hours of work.

Him: If you're gonna do it, then do it.

Love vs. Money

You can't make love to money.

You can't get a massage from coins.

A dollar bill can't caress the stress and kinks out of
your neck…only fingertips can do that.

Whispers can't be confused with jingles or jangles.

Your mind can't be seduced with salt or false
pretenses.

If you want to sit on a throne, you can do it solo.

But…it will feel more comfortable with a Queen or
King sitting on one right next to you.

Mr. Gooddbarr

Him: It's always good to connect with good people.

Me: I appreciate you. I have to give the high vibrations…most times. Well, it's never too late when it comes to meeting new (good) people. It'll only get better.

Him: See…you're doing it again lol.

Me: I'm just sending the vibes in the direction that they were designed to go. I'll put a pause on them if you want me to.

Him: Feel free to direct them as you see fit.

Me: Will do, sir. I'm listening.

Him: Good.

Me: See…see.

Him: I apologize. Please forgive me.

Me: I'll only forgive you once though.

Him: Once? I like that. You're doing it again. You're charming.

Me: I'm just trying to send a rainbow your way or maybe even a glimpse of sunshine. That's it…

Him: Sunshine? I see that I have to be really careful with you. You know exactly what to say to me.

Me: Too good. Too soon.

Him: I promise that you don't want to walk through this maze. You may start to feel a shortage of air through these pathways. Be careful where you walk because you just might run into some corners or maybe even a hidden door. Yes...too good. Too soon.

Me: Haha!! That's exactly what I'm talking about! I am a bit daring at times though, so you let me know when the time is right to brave the labyrinth.

Me: I seem to put a smile on your face again...I like that in me. I'd rather keep your mental full more than anything. If I couldn't feed your mind, then what good would I be, right? My energy can only transcend so far.

Him: Just know that I appreciate your energy. From the top all the way down I do.

Me: I'm not trying to be a Temptress to you, but I still haven't forgotten about the automatic connection that I had upon meeting you. I'll be as good as I possibly can. I'm a sensual woman. I see my sensuality as a form of artistry.

Him: Oh yes ma'am. I haven't forgotten either. I don't take that for granted. Actually, that's why I try to stay away. I know that our timing is off for one another. We both have busy lifestyles and have to focus on your studies and work. Connectivity is real. We can't tame it. We have to tame ourselves.

Me: I'm honored that you haven't forgotten. I remember trying to work on my facial expressions. I don't have a poker face for nothing in the world. You're right...we'll have to tame ourselves.

Him: Absolutely. I might forget a name, I seldom forget a face, but I never forget energy. In the back of my mind I was hoping to steal an exchange.

Me: So you were just gone steal a glimpse of energy and put it in your back pocket? I like that. I'm sure that we'll have the change for an exchange again. I'll see to it.

Him: Yes ma'am. I love your style. Save some for me.

Me: You love my style and I love your manners. I'll be sure to save some for you, but I highly doubt that it'll ever be enough. I'm willing to give it a try though.

Him: You just let me know when. I'll be ready.

Me: Just be ready when I say, "Tag…you're it!"

Him: There were moments when I was sitting and thinking about our absence from one another. I thought, "How can I miss someone that I don't even know?"

Me: Wow. Now that's real…real connection. Crazy thing is…I concur. How is that possible?

Him: You too huh? Have we been here before and the cycle is repeating? I'm unsure, but I sure do hope so.

Me: The connection was instant and automatic and now we see it's sustaining as well…feels familiar. I don't know what to make of it either.

Him: Man…instant coffee is what it was and I'm a tea drinker. It was like hot tea, honey, and a touch of cream…my favorite combination.

Me: Just an FYI, I'm stingy.

Him: Stingy you say?

Me: I study my prey and I like to eat alone.

Him: Nice. I like that. I'm here for that. I'm a man of nuances.

Me: I feel that you are. I'm saying things without saying much. Maybe you'll be able to fill in the spaces in my sentences. Perhaps. Someday. It's still too soon. Too sudden.

Him: Let us both make an agreement that we will reach out if we know we're available for each other, no matter what we spoke on before or the circumstances surrounding, we'll both commit to attempting.

Me: I promise to make some free time for you.

Him: It's our responsibility jointly.

Me: You're so cute. Yeah, I'll sign the line…geesh.

Him: Now we're both accountable going forward.

Me: Yes sir. I concur. No whips will be put on you and none on me.

Him: Feel free to do with me what you like. I surrender.

Me: Please don't tell me that. I'm really trying to work on that "other side" of me. You have no idea the kind of fun that I'm interested in.

Him: Holy shit. I can't wait. I'm in 100% compliance with WHATEVER you deem necessary. What you say goes.

Me: Have mercy on my soul and yours?

Him: Nothing will go beyond what you approve.

Me: The thoughts are an adventure in itself.

Him: You determine what we will do.

Me: Pressure. Pleasure. Pain. Which one would you like?

Him: Pressure and pleasure. Connection. Pain in a healthy dose. Whatever makes you feel whole is what I want.

Me: There are 3 keys. You only get one. Depending on which key you get, it may also unlock a treasure chest. You probably thing that I'm crazy.

Him: If I had to pick one, it would definitely be pleasure. Crazy? No. Fun? Yes. Give me more of that energy that you think that I may perceive as crazy. Please.

Me: Thank you. So pleasure is your final answer? Give you more of my perception of crazy?? Damn! This is going to be more fun than I imagined. Connection is a motherfucker.

Him: Yes.

Me: I'm thinking long and hard about what I'm going to do with us.

Him: You give me something to think about. Thank you.

Me: I want to play now, but I'll put it on hold for now.

Him: Lol…don't play with me. Next time around…no excuses.

Me: I'm going to get you every time that you're around.

Him: Good…and I'll keep coming back for more.

Me: Back to back to back.

Him: Yes. I have to see how I'm going to make things work out for the both of us.

Me: That would make me glow all over.

Him: I like how you talk. I wanna taste it. I mean…OK that's nice…that's what I meant.

Me: Funny thing…that's exactly what you were doing when you asked me to cum for you (in my mental fantasy).

Him: Yes please.

Me: I'll make sure that I fill you up. I'll burp you afterward.

Him: Yes ma'am.

Me: You can't have me sitting in a wet puddle. I don't want to be sticky right now. I'll save that for later.

Him: I'm with that.

Me: We'll see each other again soon. Just not soon enough.

Him: Exactly.

Me: You're ready to fluff your head and face on a few pillows?

Him: Yes Lawd.

Me: So you like thick milkshakes? I hope that the hole in your straw is wide enough. Let me stop being naughty.

Him: No. Don't stop.

Me: Just know that the next time, I'm definitely tying you up though. I mean…I'm definitely going to give you a tight hug when I see you.

Him: Ha!! I can't wait.

Me: I'm trying to figure out the specifics with you. I want to spread things out over a course of time in regards to our "play."

Him: Honestly, nah. There's no need to "stage" it. Let's be transparent. Honest. Free.

Me: I think that I know what you like. I most certainly want you to crawl to me.

Him: Yes. You're in control.

Me: I KNEW IT!

Him: Hahaha!!

Me: Chains and necklaces?

Him: Whatever you want.

Me: I want you to feed me too.

Him: That's easy. Tell me what you want…unrestricted. Let's be free.

Me: I primarily want to fed, sucked, and spanked.

Him: Easy…and sniffed and licked.

Me: Yes. Absolutely.

Him: Obligatory. I want to sink in it. Suffocate me in between. Bury my face in them…in IT. I wanna taste your mouth. I want you on top of me. I want you completely naked.

Me: You want your nose wedged in my ass with your eyes piercing into me while your tongue catch the drippings of my honey.

Him: Yes.

Me: Your wish is my command, sir.

Him: I wanna smell it. I want you to taste me…messy.

Me: You're gonna smell all of it. I'll suffocate you for as long as you'd like.

Him: No compromising.

Me: I'll be sure to wear little makeup so that you can paint my face.

Him: Yes. I wanna slap it on your tongue.

Me: I'm glad that we cracked the hinges of this "box."

Him: Me too. I wanna bite you. Now I'm frustrated. I want it now.

Me: You can. You can. Nibble on the tips of my ass. Sniff. Nibble. Sniff again.

Him: When are we going to do all of these things? I can't wait much longer.

Me: Do you like the way that I'm teasing you, knowing that you can't really have me?

Him: Yes and no. The thought is provoking, but I know that you're only having fun. I wanted you immediately when we first me. I already seen it.

Me: The thing is, I think that others saw it too. I didn't care. I was going to finish what I had started because I knew that I wouldn't be right not having you.

Him: We have to have each other. Fuck that.

Me: Settled. We are a part of each other now. Reconnecting the connectors. We've been here before.

Him: Just please be patient with me. I promise to give you whatever you want.

I give em a lil bit and they want a lot.

Love Prison

I'm sitting here on this stiff cold bench behind bars.

I stand up, looking through the metal pipes, awaiting your arrival.

I don't see you.

I sit back down.

My feet are tapping the ground.

I'm getting impatient.

What time is it?

How long have I been here?

Has it been minutes?

Has it been days?

Months?

Weeks?

I'm weak.

I have a headache.

I'm nauseous.

Have I even eaten today?

Have I quenched my thirst with water?

My thoughts are drenched in you.

I see you swimming up there…in my mind.

I'm trapped in this place and you're trapped in me.

Instructor

Him: Someone tell this beautiful woman that I have a crush on her. She is loyal, beautiful energy, and spirit. I am honored to be connected with you.

Me: I will tell her, but only under one condition. You ready? You will have to tell the royal Emperor that I noticed him for many many years, but his eyes were not open to seeing me. I first spotted him at a diner. I was enjoying tea and breakfast in the distance. I'm honored that he finally found me. I just don't know how to feel about it due to the timing. But the connection that I feel for him still hasn't gone away.

Him: Wow, I never knew that. How beautiful is that? Once blind, but I can promise that I have sight now and see you as clear as day. Well, you tell the beautiful Toni that her artistic crafts created thoughts within me. The timing not right, yet the connection still exists? How should we proceed with such? Explore or admire from afar?

Me: Yes, I sure did. Oh what a lovely sight it was. I thought to myself, "This is a beautiful man. Not just physically, but spiritually. I need to know him." I yearn to know him. You are correct…yoga does that quite often. To be honest, I also told myself, "I want him." Is that such a naughty thing to say? Hmmm? Explore or admire from a far? That's such a tough call. There are needs and there are wants. Sometimes we need what we want.

Him: Yeah, I move quite privately…just work to be better is my motto. I had no idea such a beautiful spirit had such energy for me, which makes it even better now that we're connected. By the way, I've heard people speak on doing yoga, but it didn't have the same effect as when you told me. It's not naughty, but it can become naughty with the right energy…fun and pleasurable as well. When you meet a desire, want, and need rolled all up in one, what's created is often beyond words. A connection many only dream about. It's an experience most can fathom. All you'll realize as you recover from your sprinkler system going off is that the connection is real. Oh…and I'd love to watch you get your yoga on one day. Some of those initial thoughts I had may run into a reality.

Me: I'm trying to keep my gasps low and quiet. I'm smelling the aromas of incense and tea tree oils. No lie, I'm taking a bath as I was reading your words. My mind is in another place right now. I can tell that you live a private lifestyle, which I admire. I'm only attracted to guys who keep a low profile. You're also an Educator. I wouldn't mind if you taught me in more ways than one. I'd like to read all of you and your works. Can you teach me? Can I sit and watch you? You can help me with some of my yoga stretches if you'd like or you can just watch me. Are you married? Single? What's your relationship status if you don't mind me asking?

Him: So you just gonna plant the vision of you in the bath in my mind like that, huh? Now I'm thinking of taking a face towel and taking my time drying you off. I definitely wouldn't mind teaching you or having long private tutor sessions. I have plenty for you to read. It's a lot of knowledge to swallow. I definitely would watch and then help you stretch. I could see how flexible you are up close and personal. I'm single, love…still searching. I have a few errands to run, is it okay if we pick up this conversation shortly?

Me: See…see, you are so wrong to do me like that. You started first when you mentioned the sprinkler system. I just tagged you back. (You gone get it for real if you keep flirting with me.) Yes, we can continue this conversation later. What's your number?

He gives me the number.

Him: We can finish our conversation and yes, love…I can guarantee that your sprinkler system will go off (multiple times).

Me: Hello, Professor. It's always the quiet ones that you have to watch. You can continue once you get settled.

Him: Will do. Are you still relaxing in the tub?

Me: Yes, but I don't want to wrinkle myself, so I'm getting out now.

Him: That picture in my thoughts still intrigues me. You're welcome to share some of that energy…wrinkled or not.

Me: You are a wild one. I thought that I was bad. You are going to be so bad for me…I can feel it in my pelvis! I'm telling "her" to hush!

Him: Sounds like we're gonna have fun. As far as your pelvis…she ain't gotta hush. Tell her that I said, "Hey, Ms. Lady."

Me: By the way…I don't send pics, but feel free to send any that you'd like to. I don't mind seeing some glimpses of you.

Him: Don't worry, you can send them when you're comfortable. It seems that we've got catching up to do. Question.

Me: You're that confident, huh? It's one of my rules…no sending of pics for me. What's your question?

Me: I just knew deep down that you would find me. It's just surreal that we both find this deep connection for one another. So close, yet so far.

Him: Why wouldn't I be, love? Seems we were connected before we connected. I respect your rule, but I know that it's gonna be fun breaking it. I don't cause trouble and I guard privacy. I just was going to ask what were your rules and regulations? I don't want to cause chaos in your life.

Me: You're right…you radiate with confidence. The connection was already planted. I just hit my own hand for not knowing better. So here's the thing. Well, I've always wanted more than one. So dating can be kind of tough. I will still be respectful to whomever I deal with, but they will have to know that they will not be the only one. I'm telling you because I want to be honest with you. I'm a free spirit, but I still want to show my main respect. I also don't like denying myself guilty pleasure every now and then either. I'm selective with it, though, and not reckless. I want to learn you more. We can start out slow since I'm testing your waters. As far as sending messages/calling, I'd prefer it be before my bedtime. I like my beauty sleep. I'd prefer it to be before 9 p.m. I'm usually settled in by that time. My planner is pretty full, but I always make time for what I really want. What does your schedule usually look like?

Him: I respect that. We can take it slow and grow. I'll stay within the respected time zone. My schedule flexes around much, but we can make things work.

Me: Quick question before I settle in. Where will we meet for our "talks"?

Him: Where you wanna meet? I can get a private room for private discussions.

Me: My brown skin is blushing. How is that moving slow? You basically said in so many words, "Fuck it...I'm just gone go all in."

Him: LMAO! My crush is feeling me...what am I supposed to do?!

Me: If you don't stop. You forgot that I see more than you think I do. I know that the ladies love you too. I also know about your "Harem."

Him: LMAO! Harem though?? There's nothing wrong with being loved...especially by your crush.

Me: I'm intelligent too ya know.

Him: Oh...I do know that.

Me: To society, having more than one loving on you is wrong. For people like us? No. I'll still blow you a few kisses from a far...even on your worse behaviors.

Him: I don't care what society gotta say. They don't dictate me.

Me: Exactly. That's why I'm attracted to you so much. I'm the same way. There's nothing traditional about me at all. When I mentioned harem...that's what I meant by worse behavior.

Him: Yeah, it's probably why it was meant for us to connect...energy doesn't lie. Me just remembering you needing a couple of hours to get yourself situated...I wanted to arrive a little early.

Me: Man...when you walked through that door I wanted to hold you so tight and throw yo ass to the floor. I knew it wasn't appropriate, so I kept quiet for the most part. I didn't really want you to leave. Our chemistry was so pleasantly calm. I wanted to talk to you all day.

Him: You should've. I had the same energy. I just didn't want to cause any chaos. You could've asked me to stay a little longer just to talk or show me those yoga moves.

Me: I don't think that would've been a good idea. A few times I wanted to invite you over. See…there I go drifting off into my deep naughty thoughts.

Him: I like your naughtiness. You have my contact and can invite me when you're ready. You're overdue for a long study session. You need at least a couple lessons at a time.

Me: I have my own place and I live alone. Don't make me tuck you away in my "closet." I've also been waiting for you to put me on your bike for a long time. I don't want to wait any more summers to ride on it…put my "stinger" right on the seat.

Him: I hear that…real naughty action.

Me: Absolutely. I'll keep you in mind. We'll catch up soon.

Him: This is going to be fun.

Me: Just be careful with me. I'm sure that you'll never get enough. You'll always be hungry. By the way, I'm clean. I get checked every year.

I send him a copy of my STD test results. I'm an advocate of having healthy clean sex.

Him: I'll be careful with you. I'm willing to get tested too and show you my results. We'll enjoy each other completely. You're definitely going to be dessert.

Me: Ahem…so I actually prefer to be eaten. That's high priority. Will you promise to suck me until my sprinkler system goes off? She is ready as we speak for some of that. I'm about to get ready for bed. Goodnight, Professor.

Him: You don't have to ask. Just don't stop me when I'm enjoying myself. Good night, love.

Several days later.

Me: Good morning, Professor.

Him: Good morning, love. How are you doing on this beautiful Monday?

Me: Thank you. The sky was multi-colored and beautiful when I was out, so I'm off to a great start. How are things on your end of the rainbow?

Him: Everything is peaceful. I had an early workout, my caffeine, and I'm ready to shower and get my day started. Today will be a fruitful and productive day. I'm still waiting to schedule a yoga session or quality study time.

Me: I'm trying not to "cheese" too hard around these people while reading your messages. I'm just visualizing you in your morning routine. I love how you speak…even via text. Your time with me will come soon. It would be tonight if things were in alignment for it. I have some important things to tend to right now. Maybe we could plan for the next few weeks to have our much needed time in. When time does permit, I'll definitely be making time for you and I to connect.

Him: Forgive me, but my energy will keep a smile on you. Tonight? That could be fun aligning. We can put plans together. I would like to taste your flavor tea and you can see how strong mine is.

Me: I think that you tried to make my hands shake and my spine catch a quiver. I see what you did there, sir.

Him: …and you could send me that smile that I put on you. Share the sunshine on this side of the rainbow. That's only the beginning. Just wait until I taste that tea of yours. Every sip will cause the cup to shake.

Me: You want what you want, huh? I'm going to make you wait for that. Since you did mention your shower, I'd like to have a peek behind those shower curtains please and thanks. I think that you're seriously trying to make me throb.

Him: You sharing that sunshine will brighten my day.

Me: I'm waiting…

Him: If it's throbbing now, the muscle memory that I create is gonna be even more intense.

Me: None of my work is going to ever get done now. I'm about to go home and reevaluate my day. I can't with you right now.

Him: Go on and get your work done. Just squeeze your thighs together when she throbs. That's proof you can feel me already. I've gotta question though.

Me: I'm still getting back to my posh self. I should have known better dealing with you. I'm scared to ask what the question is…but what is it?

Him: Does your tea start to overflow as you taste other's tea?

Me: My tea can overflow just from the sight of other's tea or even simply milk chocolate. You'll have to see the drippings for yourself.

Him: It ain't gone hurt you to rub her just a lil bit while you're at work is it? Oh our tea time will be great. I'll enjoy every sip until it spills over and then some.

Me: I do have on a skirt, so I could probably even do it at my desk, huh? Or I could tuck you under for you to do it for me…is that a possibility?

Him: Now wouldn't that be fun? Gently rubbing her as you pretend to be writing something…spreading your thighs open slowly for better positioning. Also allowing your skirt to ride up slowly. Here, kitty kitty…make her purr. I don't think that you could take me being under your desk. Fun thought though. Maybe we can role-play that later on in life and see.

Me: Breathe…just breathe is what I'm telling myself right now. I knew that this was going to happen. Just wait until I see you, sir.

Him: What happened? Sounds like you're gonna thank me when you see me.

Me: You are so wrong, yet so right for me to enjoy. Are you going to make me wait for my shower pic?

Him: Yeah, we're gonna have a lot of fun. I thought about it, but someone didn't want to share my sunshine on this side of the rainbow.

Me: Can I at least have a pic of you looking into the camera? Pretty please?

Him: I'm open to doing that, but with a big beautiful smile and all the greatness we've shared just today, I was told that I'd have to wait. On a cloudy day like this, sunshine would be great to have on this side of the rainbow. Are you going to be my sunshine when I need it?

Me: I thought that you were going to let me have my way with you? Don't get shy in the first quarter. We still have a long game ahead of us.

Him: You must understand love…I respect the rules. But I need certain energy in order to give certain energy. You closed a door, so if you want it open, the door must swing from your side. You can't pull on a door that says "push."

Me: I guess that I'll just have to wait until I can physically have you in my presence before I can see the face that I admired so much.

Him: We're both worth the wait. Seems you're not willing to give the energy you wanna receive. Well…not in the beginning that is. I'm pretty sure I'll have no problem with getting such energy. Doubt I'll even have to ask. We'll get there. Until then…rub, Ms. Kitty. Also, tell her that I can't wait to taste her and feel your thighs around my head…as you shake like it's 10 degrees below zero.

Me: So you just gone make sure that you pull me back into that space? All right, I see how it's gone be. My fall will have more than just leaves falling. The panties will be too…I'm sure of it. Summer can end today already.

He sends a song to me.

Me: I see you are still picking with me. I'm gone tear ya ass up when I get my fingertips on you. I'm leaving fingerprints on EVERYTHING.

Him: Didn't you mention something about tonight?

Me: It was wishful thinking. I should've said something earlier when I first encountered you. We could've had our tea time in by now.

Him: We have time to make up.

He sends me another song.

Me: I haven't heard that one. Like how did I miss it lol? "When I melt in your mouth…Almond Joy." "Licking his fingers begging for more." "You like this flavor…try it out." Mind is gone right now! I keep thinking about how I'm gone get you. I want it to be unexpected. No planning. I just want you to be ready come next week.

He sends me yet another song.

Me: That's the type of song that makes me want to hover my thick-ass thighs over you and just wind my hips while I'm just rocking on the "tip." I haven't heard it before, but I like it.

Him: Just know the stick shift has a big jerk to it. Be careful. It doesn't sit still. A deep clutch may make you lose control.

Me: I absolutely love your wordplay!!

Him: Wait until you find out that it ain't just words.

Me: So where do you prefer to eat your food? The dinner table is nice, but what about the other areas of the house? Trucks? Cars? Parks? Dugouts? Where? By the way, I'm used to a lot of movement. I like rugged rides with tinted windows.

Him: I make the best meal in any location. If you're gonna feed me, don't be afraid of my big appetite. I might have to extend the back of the trunk of your vehicle…make room for the clutch.

Me: I'm a juicy girl in all areas. You just make sure that you'll be able to retain all those fluids. You may need an extra container. I might have to open one of those back windows. I'm sure that your feet will be jumping from the convulsions. They'll need space to move around. I'm make sure to keep bouncing until it hurts you.

Him: The juicier the better. I have great swimming techniques and deep diving strokes. If you can cause a big splash, then keep bouncing. The second laps will have your toes throwing up gang signs.

Me: These people are looking at me because I keep giggling over here. My concentration is off now…thanks. We will see who can actually keep their word.

Him: Let's see if you can keep that same energy after your sprinkler system goes off.

Me: Would you stop? (My focus is off at this point.) One more thing…if I'm not on my back, while you're eating my lotus flower bomb, then I only prefer to ride your stick shift. I like to be in full control mode. Okay? Okay…we'll talk later.

Him: I won't stop just because you reach climax. I'll introduce you to a higher and deeper level of the "Yoniverse." I'll be your "asstronaut." You're gonna feed me however I wanna eat it. Even when I let you in the driver seat, I'll still have my hands on the wheel. This ain't your original ride.

Me: OMG!!! If you could get me to that place, I might just fall in love with you!!

Him: It ain't an if about it…

Me: I'm kinda scared…just a little bit. (I can't lie)

Him: FYI...I've watched the complete Kama Sutra. You're gonna get exactly what you've been waiting for.

Me: I look forward to it, "Mr. King of Love." So have you had two women before? How many women have you had at once?

Him: I've only had two at once. I probably could've had more, but I didn't want to bite off more than I could chew. Which position would you prefer to be in?

Me: Would you want me with another woman or all to yourself? My favorite position is me riding. That's the only way that I like to have sex. I either like to ride from the front or like to ride backwards...both will work for me. Also, I like for my "twins" to be sucked while I'm riding it or me kissing while I'm riding.

Him: Both... We can have private yoga sessions and sessions with another woman. I'm sure that I can introduce you to other positions that'll be to your liking. I definitely wanna see what your ride game like since it's your favorite. You don't have to ask...those twins of yours will be getting a lot of attention.

Me: I've actually never been in a "threesome." It's crazy because as of late, I've been attracting more women than men. This young lady has been on my head about tasting me. The problem is, I'm not attracted to women sexually. I like the aggression and the strength of a man.

Him: Well, I can bring balance to that. We can share that experience together. With both of our energies, we're sure to keep it fun and exciting. She may not be ready for us.

Me: You just had to turn the dial just a few more notches, don't ya? What did I walk into?!

Him: Ain't no reason not to, love. Keep it hot and exciting. We're gonna have fun and enjoy each other fully. Is there a way that you can sneak me under your desk at work? I wanna feel your thighs around my face.

Me: Is that how you'll have your head...tilted up and under my dress?

Him: You gotta dress on?

Me: I wear a dress 99.9% of the time.

Him: Gimme that under-the-desk view. Handle your business. The yoga session is gonna be fun. I wanna cum visit you at work one day if you can get away with it.

Me: I'm under surveillance at work, otherwise I'd bring you every day.

Him: Respected. I'll just have you cum out on your work break and get that throat poked.

Me: Lol oh...I almost forgot that I was talking to the "Love Kinggg." You better be about that action too. Otherwise we're going to box. How did we get here? We moved so fast.

Him: I'm definitely about that action, love. Fruits for breakfast...you can swallow every drop. We've been here. We're finally catching up on lost time. That under the desk view got me ready to special deliver you to my face. Could you really contain yourself with me under your desk? Your legs above my shoulders? My arms under your desk, but around you...slowly kissing Ms. Kitty?

Me: I'm multitasking, but most of my mental energy is still focused on you. I have people around me and my hopes are that they aren't glancing at my phone screen. You are right. I feel like you were already mine. Only thing is that I'll have to wrap my mind around sharing you. I'm stingy. I want your arms wrapped around my waist and me pushing my yoni closer to your face while I drip and rain on your beard and mustache.

Him: Handle your business, love. Don't worry, you're gonna have fun sharing. Probably more than me. With all of our energy, we must have her sprung off rip. I can't wait to taste you and see if you can handle my appetite. When you're free, bring Ms. Kitty to the light.

Me: I'm sure that I will have fun. She is yearning like crazy right now. I've waited this long, I guess some days won't hurt my heart too much. You will be notified the moment that I have some time all to myself…to give to you.

He sends me a link to a song.

Me: Who knew that you'd be putting me on to the greatness? It rocks nice…has a blues feel to it. I listen to music most of my day. Keep 'em cumin, please and thanks.

Him: I'm gone put yo royal ass on a lot of things, love. You're going to enjoy this journey.

Me: I don't know whether to call you my professor or the Love King.

Him: It's up to you and what you're feeling at the time.

Him: Ms. Kitty needs to cum and get kissed on.

Me: You want to be kissed ASAP. I do too. I swear the timing is off though. So many activities going on. I'll have some free time coming up within the next few weeks, so I'll make time for you. What days/times work best for you? I keep thinking about that office action. It's stuck. Do you have an office that we can visit next week?

He sends me another song link.

Me: I like this. Professors can be so tempting. I'll be good today.

Him: Rub those thighs for me.

Me: They'll be rubbing against your cheekbones soon. I'll let you take a few gasps of air…maybe 2 or 3.

Him: Don't worry I have a technique that'll have you spreading your legs open like a yoga stretch. You wearing a dress?

Me: I have on lingerie. I'm about to get dressed though.

Him: Sneak peek?

Me: All I see is brown sugar and honey.

Him: Oh really? I can pull up and see right now if you ain't in camera-friendly mode.

Me: I could possibly be a "scratch and sniff" and put it right up under your nose.

Him: Well, a sneak and peek will do till we link later this week.

Me: Will you give me a sneak peek too?

Him: Maybe. I thought about it last week, but that front view under the desk never came thru.

Me: I need a yes in order for me to show reciprocity.

Him: It ain't a yes. You told me you'd do something last week and didn't honor it. You got some making up to do, love.

Me: I didn't agree to such a thing. You were asking about coming to the job after the pic was sent. I see what you're doing. I guess neither of us will be getting our way today.

Him: It's cool, love. You don't have to send me a sneak peek if you are not up to it. I do like when one honors their word. Do enjoy the rest of your day.

Me: Likewise, sweetie. Have a peaceful day. I think that you're in my psyche. I dreamt of you early this morning.

Him: Sounds like a great way to start the day off.

Me: I'm scared of you.

Him: I know. When are you ready to face your fears?

Me: I'm not sure exactly.

He mentions having a threesome again.

Him: You ready for a yoga session? I'm about to get dressed and I'm going to text you. I want to find out how the session is going to go today.

Me: No, you're not about to set me up with one of those sessions. Not gonna happen.

Him: I want a private session with you. We've got some catching up to do.

Me: Is that a regular thing for you?

Him: I'm trying to have one with you. Do you think that you'll have fun?

Me: I don't think that I'd ever be ready for something like that, so you'd be bored with me.

Him: Don't worry, I can bring the fun outta you.

Me: It could possibly be a lovely sight because of the artistry, but I'm not sexually attracted to women.

Him: Yet...we can still have fun with a woman who's attracted to you.

Me: It's the same, silly.

Him: Naw, not if you enjoy yourself. But anyway, I still need to have a one-on-one study session with you before we get into all of that.

Me: Yeah, if we can ever catch up with our busy lifestyles.

Him: We will. We will or I'm going to have to cum see you on your lunch break.

Me: Now that would be fun.

Him: I can still cum to you. All that you have to do is give me the word.

Me: If I was giving you a heads up, it could've been this morning.

Him: I wanna cum taste that kitty. You should've hit me up and said that you needed an early study session.

Me: I was ready to burst all week. You probably could've had at least 4 sessions by now.

Him: You should've called the professor to cum to class.

Me: I wanted to so bad, but I thought you were busy or probably changed your mind.

Him: Don't think for me, love. I was behind schedule, but I never changed my mind about linking up with you.

Me: My apologies. I'll check in the next time if I feel that you're behind schedule.

Him: No free time this weekend?

Me: My plans aren't going how I mapped them out for the weekend, so I'm unsure.

Him: Hmmm. Well, if a quick session pops up, don't hesitate to hit me up, love.

Me: I most certainly will, Professor.

So I run into him at an event. I receive a message that reads: I see you.

Me: I don't see you.

Him: Blind.

I finally see where he's sitting.

Him: You are smiling so bright. Your smile made the sun come from behind the clouds. Everything literally moved and lit up. Let me get an under-the-dress view.

Me: Later. I'm sweaty right now.

Him: So. You should've let me touch you scary.

Me: You are all in public acting a fool.

Him: Don't be shook. I ain't going to blow your cover, but we can still have fun in public. Pull that dress back for me.

Me: I love public places, by the way. The timing is just not right. I especially love the dugouts. I love baseball.

Him: It is definitely right. A lil touch is not gonna hurt just get you a lil excited. Next time, I want you to get in my car.

I decide to meet with him.

Me: Will you be available for me?

Him: I can make that happen. You ready to have some fun?

Me: See…you're being silly again. I'll be leaving in 10 min. Where would you like to meet?

He gives me the location for a nature walk.

Me: I know where it is. I'm about to head out shortly.

Him: All right, I'll meet you there.

Me: I'm here.

Him: Pull down on me.

So when we meet, he smiles and I smile back at him. My smile is a little bit brighter than his, so I'm working on keeping my composure. He can sense that I am elated but uneasy at the same time. He immediately grabs my hand and locks his with mine.

He asks, "Are you ready for our walk?"

I respond, "Yes, I am...let's go."

It is an instant romance. The night is uniquely beautiful. The trees are in full bloom. I can smell the fresh flowers, which hold the night's light dew. The air is crisp. There is low lighting from the moon's reflection and from the few streetlights that are lit. I have no idea what route we'll walk, but he knows foot by foot where we are going to go. I let him lead. It is one of the few times that I have followed. I'm usually the one setting the rules...for almost everything.

I say, "What if deer run up on us?"

He begins to laugh and says, "Don't worry, love...I'm here to protect you," as he holds my hand tighter and gives me a forehead kiss. We continue our walk. We stand there for a few moments and take in some breaths of fresh air. He gets behind me and holds on to me. He asks, "Are you ready?"

I say, "Ready for what?"

He says, "Just walk and I'll direct you."

I continue to walk the pathway. In my mind, the path seems long for the simple fact that I don't know where I am going. I can hear shuffles of small animals rumbling through the woods. I am trying to keep my composure. I love nature, but when you can't see what's in front of you, it can make things slightly edgy. He keeps reassuring me that I'll be safe and that he will stand in the way if anything comes toward us. My body begins to relax as I listen to his words.

Shortly after we walk the path, he directs my body toward the grass. He then gets in front of me and grabs my arms from behind his waist. He puts my arms around his waist and now he's walking in front of me. I put my forehead in the center of his back and start to look down as we're walking. I start to rub my right cheek against his back and begin to hold him even tighter. As my cheek is against his body, I look over and notice the moon. I begin to smile.

With me not being able to see where I'm going, he says, "Are you ready?" again.

I say, "Ready? Ready…for what?"

He says, "Have a seat at the table."

I take a deep breath and begin to smile. At this moment, I'm intrigued but nervous at the same time. I'm wearing a dress. I walk around the table and proceed to sit on the bench.

He says, "I didn't say have a seat on the bench. I said have a seat at the table…on top of it."

I replied, "Oh…so you want me to sit on the table for our conversation?"

He says, "Yeah…something like that. I'd like to talk to you and 'her'…Ms. Kitty."

I then look to the side, smile, and proceed to have a seat at the table. He tells me to slide down a little more to the end of the table. He grips my waist and pulls me closer to him. He looks up at me and smiles. He wraps his arms around me and lays his head on my lap. I can feel the air from his nose hitting my skin. His breathing is heavy. He lifts his head up and puts his hand on my stomach. He pushed me lightly so that my back lies against the table. He tucks his forearms behind the folds of my legs and pulls my body down so that my ass is slightly hanging off the table. He releases one of my legs, so now it is dangling over the table and my foot isn't touching the ground. One leg is still resting on one of his arms.

He then takes his other hand and flexes my leg up toward the sky. I begin to flex my leg and point my foot. He begins to caress my stomach muscles and my legs. He starts at the top of my leg and then his hand begins to stroke the back of my hamstring and calf muscle. He flexes my leg further down, so that my knee is almost meeting my breast. He then says, "You are flexible…my goodness, Queen."

He brings my leg back up toward him. He grabs my ankle and starts to softly kiss all sides and angles of my ankle. From my ankle, he moves toward my calf and begins to kiss and lick on that too. He moves down to my hamstring. Once he reaches my hamstring, he drapes my leg to the side. With his other hand, he slowly moves my dress up and brings it from underneath my ass to my waist. He takes one of his fingers and moves one side of my panties to the other side of my pussy lips. He uses one of his fingers to glide up and down my clit and rests the tip of his fingers in my opening. He says, "I'm going to start calling you Tsunami…that's exactly what you feel like. You are wet as fuck!" He then slides my panties off and puts them in his pocket.

Shortly after he tells me that, he says, "Oh yeah…you're definitely about to be dessert for tonight. I'm not going to stop until I'm all the way full."

My eyes start to feel heavy and begin to close on their own. He is most certainly practicing what he was preaching months prior.

I occasionally look to the sky. It is almost as if I am seeing the stars winking at me and saying, "I see you, girl…let him do his thing!" The sky has a personality all its own at times. The trees surround us. I can see them swaying in the dim lighting that we have. The trees even know what to do…they begin to cool us down. I promise the animals know what he is doing to me, too.

I can't keep my noises low. I've never been a singer, but I feel like one that night. My pitches are so loud. So loud, in fact, I think that the bats are going to start flying over me. I can hear them making noises almost reflecting the noises that I am making. I remember the twists and turns of my body. Every time I try to move, he keeps pulling me back for the secretions of my yoni to drop in his mouth like raindrops falling into a puddle of water.

He lifts up and I'm trying hard to come back to my normal self. My eyes are still heavy, but I eventually keep them open. He says, "Sit up and don't say anything." I lightly laugh and ask why he said that. He says there are others in the woods with us. I think that he's joking with me. I then see a light from a flashlight. I guess my moans didn't alert just the animals, but others as well. He tells me to slowly get off the table and to hold his hand and let him lead us out.

We walk and then eventually make it out of the woods and are clear from others. We both begin to laugh. He says, "I told you that I got you. Did you enjoy yourself? The deer were out there talking about the jungle noises you were making." I tell him that I did in fact enjoy myself.

He walks me to my vehicle, kisses me on my cheek, and says to me, "I think that you're going to need these." He is holding up the panties that he had in his pocket. I have completely forgotten that I am no longer wearing any.

I tell him, "Thanks for spending time with me. You were patient with me and I appreciate you for that. I'm going to home now and shower and head to bed. You get some rest."

* * *

Some of the most memorable words ever said to me by a man were: "Don't ever try to get skinny. Men will be with the big girls, while the skinny ones will be focused on their weight."

No Comparison

No complexion is as beautifully bronzed as yours.

No slant of eyes that see through me the way that
you do.

You mean everything to me.

I mean more to you than I will ever know.

No kiss can touch me without even making a
connection.

No thump of the heart sounds equal to yours.

No touch can submit shivers the way that you do.

No one is capable of deciphering the pleasure that
you give.

No comparison.

Peppermint Candies

We're sitting in the back seat listening to music and catching up with laughter and conversation. I want my breath to be fresh at all times, so I reach in my purse and grab some mints. I ask him if he wants one too. I say, "These mints are strong and powerful."

He says, "Yeah, they sure are," and starts to laugh. I tell him how mints have a tendency to have a cooling yet heating sensation in the mouth or when it comes in contact with the skin. I start to kiss him on his lips after a few moments, with the mint still in my mouth. After it melts, I decide to reach for more. This time, I put two mints in my mouth at once. I start to kiss him again, with the mints still in my mouth. As I'm doing this, I begin to unbuckle his belt. I tell him that I promise to keep both of my mints in my mouth. I pull out his manhood and slide the mints under my tongue on each side. I put him in my mouth. He grabs my hair and makes a ponytail for me with his hands. I can barely talk because my mouth is now full with him and candy. I try to make out how sweet everything tastes. I also say how cooling my mouth feels.

He moans the words, "Shit…I'm feeling cool too. It's almost hot, but it feels so fucking good. Got damn!! I've never had this done to me before." His hands relax a bit, loosening the ponytail. At this point, my hair is spread all over his lap. My face is fully hidden under my hair. He grabs the center of my head and pushes it down. My mouth feels even more full at this point. All of the wetness from my mouth is now dripping all over his torso and his jeans. I'm letting it get messy…on purpose. The more that I slurp, the harder he moans. I reach around to put my hand on top of his. I push my hand on his, directing him to push my head down even harder. He does it…he pushes down harder…and harder.

I begin to moan and maneuver my body so that I'm sitting on my knees perpendicular to his body. I make sure to hike my ass up and he notices it. I'm wearing a dress, as I do most times. He takes the other hand and lifts my dress over my ass. He's now rubbing and slapping on my ass with one hand and with the other still pushing my head down. I start to move my head up and down and giving occasional moves of my lower body. He's about to burst. I start to go even faster. He then releases. I hold on to it in my mouth. I open the car door and spit it out on the pavement. I bring myself back inside and start to smile at him.

At this moment, he's still trying to catch his breath. He can barely keep his eyes open. He's slumped with his head on the backseat headrest. His arms and hands are also slumped to the side of him with the palms open and faced upward. His fingers looked limp. His manhood is now limp as well with drips glistening from it. He is conquered. He is taken down. I send him on his way. I'm satisfied seeing him satisfied.

The next morning he says, "Hello, Ms. Icebreaker."

I tell him, "Yes, it is I. I gave you winter in August. I turned you into a snowman."

My Pen

I fall in love with you daily. You arouse me. I fall victim to your tempo. Your cursive curvatures are surrendering. Your penmanship is your signature move. You wash my emotions with you. The caress that you give me is tighter than any hug a man has ever given me. My cries are dried up by the leaking of your ink. You surround my fingertips, letting them know that they will forever be protected in you. The secrets of my fingerprints will never be told. Your tube is full for me…never empty. I see you smile each time I pick you up. You like how I care about you too. I kiss you with each grip. You're spoiled…you cry when I have to lay you down. I give in and pick you back up. I thump you on my forehead when I'm lost in my thoughts. You kiss me and then put my notions back on track.

I've had poor men and I've had rich men. The only thing that they'll all ever have in common is that I'll see them all as toys.

www.ingramcontent.com/pod-product-compliance
Lightning Source LLC
Chambersburg PA
CBHW071837020726
47502CB00004B/1408